JORDAN SONNENBLICK

AFTER
EVER
AFTER

SCHOLASTIC INC.

This book was originally published in hardcover by Scholastic Press in 2010.

ISBN 978-0-545-72287-2

16 15 14 13   18 19/0

Printed in the U.S.A.   40
This edition first printing, May 2014

The text type was set in Gill Sans.
The display type was hand-lettered by Nina Goffi.
Book design by Nina Goffi and Marijka Kostiw

TO EMILY PENROSE,
THE BRAVEST KID WHO
EVER SET FOOT
IN MY CLASSROOM

ACKNOWLEDGMENTS

Special thanks to Susan Shaw, R.N., M.S., P.N.P., and the late Nan S. Songer, M.S., for urging me to tell the story of late effects, for sharing their vast expertise, and most of all, for showing by shining example that in the battle against cancer, fighting IS winning.

TABLE OF CONTENTS

FOUR YEARS AGO

I'm in fourth grade. One day, I'm sitting in my seat in class, minding my own business. I'm kind of quiet, but everyone knows exactly who I am: Jeffrey Alper, That Boy Who Had Cancer. There isn't a kid in the grade who hasn't eaten spaghetti at the church hall's annual Alper Family "Fun-Raiser" Dinner, or gotten dragged to a high school jazz band concert in my honor, or — God help me — bought a Save Jeffrey T-shirt. If you were me, you'd try to keep a low profile, too.

The door opens, and the school counselor walks in, followed by a scrawny kid on crutches. As the counselor starts a whispering powwow with our teacher, the kid sidesteps around her, and I gasp. He's bald. He's muttering angrily to himself. And there's a huge, curving red scar across the entire side of his head.

There follows the kind of awkward silence that, by the time we're in eighth grade, would probably cause some wise guy to say, "Whoa, dude! Awkward silence!" But we're still in fourth grade, so we just sit there and squirm until the teacher turns to us and says, "Boys and girls, we have a new student joining us today. His name is Thaddeus Ibsen. Do you remember when we had that talk last week about how we were going to welcome a new class-mate? Well, here he is! Thaddeus is going to need our help in becoming a member of our classroom family, and I know I can count on each and every one of you. Now, Thaddeus, why don't you come on over here and take a seat next to ... let's see ... Jeffrey Alper?"

Why is she putting the new kid next to me? Suddenly, I get it. I don't remember the special talk she supposedly had with the class last week, but then again, I'm absent a lot. Also, I don't always catch on so fast, but this time, I put two and two together. It takes a moment for the counselor to pull out the chair next to mine, for the new kid to maneuver himself into it, and for class to start up again. As soon as the teacher begins telling us about our next social studies assignment, I lean over and whisper, "Hi, I'm Jeffrey. I had cancer, too."

He looks at me like I'm a particularly loathsome slice of school-lunch meat loaf and says, "Wow, congratulations! What do you want, a medal?"

That's how I meet my best friend.

THE END...

Well, for what it's worth, I'm here. I never knew it was possible to feel so numb on such a big day. I'm sitting in my hot, sticky gown, trying to keep my big, stupid-looking square hat from tilting and sliding off my head completely. It doesn't help that the metal folding chair I'm on has been baking in the sun for hours. I stare at the sweat-drenched neck pimples of the kid in front of me, but really I'm not looking at anything.

In fact, because I'm me, I'm spacing out. My mom always says, "Give Jeffrey ten seconds, and he'll find *something* to wonder about." And today, I have more material than usual. For example, why is everybody staring so hard at me? I guess I should be used to it by now, but I'm not. People used to stare at me enough when I was just one half of the Cancer Twins, but things have hit a whole new level since the relapse. And my long ride. The whole state testing fiasco. The lawsuit threat, and the Great Eighth-Grade Walkout.

Now I am not just Jeffrey Alper, struggling eighth grader. Since all this stuff has hit the fan, for the second time in my life, I am Jeffrey Alper, Official Town Cause.

Go, me.

If you want to know how this thing started, I'll tell you. It was right at the beginning of the year, in Miss Palma's English class. She gave each kid (except me and Tad) a marble notebook, and told us that she would assign journal topics several days each week as class warm-up exercises. Then she told us our first topic: The Most Annoying Thing in the World. I opened my laptop and got right to work:

When I was four years old, I was diagnosed with cancer. The treatment lasted almost three years, and it was rough. I lost all my hair, which used to be blond and curly and really cool. When it grew back in, it was brown and straight and really dorky. I remember being tired all the time, and having bruises all over my body. Oh, and I used to throw up pretty often. I still have the scar on one side of my chest from where the doctors implanted my chemotherapy port, too.

I don't remember most of the details, but I know that being treated for leukemia was torture. The funny thing is, the treatment is nothing compared to what happens after you're "cured." And that's the most annoying thing in the world: They tell you how lucky you are to be cured, like you've escaped a death sentence. But being a cancer survivor can be a life sentence all its own.

On the last day of my cancer treatment, the hospital people threw a little party with cake and ice cream. Everybody was hugging and laughing, but my mom looked sad the whole time. On the whole two-hour ride home from Philadelphia, I tried to sleep. It was hard because my brother, Steven, wouldn't stop blabbing on and on about his girlfriend, Annette, but finally, Steven and I must both have dozed off. When we were maybe half an hour from home, I woke up. My parents were talking in the front seat, and it sounded like my mother might have been crying. Dad was being his usual impatient self.

"What do we do now?" Mom asked.

"What do you mean, 'what do we do now?' We get off the turnpike and make a left."

"Ha-ha. I mean . . . what do we do now?"

"I don't know, honey. Maybe we go home and live happily ever after."

"But we don't know if Jeffrey will stay healthy. You know he won't even officially be out of the woods for two more years. But there we were, eating cake and pretending everything's perfect. It just seems . . . wrong."

"So what are you saying? Should we sit around wearing black until Jeffrey's almost ten? Look, I don't mean to snap at you. Really, I don't. It's just . . . we have to put this behind us. The way I see it, we don't have a whole lot of other choices."

Looking back, it seems pretty weird that Dad was the one saying we should all live happily ever after. I guess saying it and doing it are two different things, or he wouldn't hate me so much now.

"Time!" Miss Palma called. "Jeffrey Alper, did you hear me? It's time to stop writing now."

Apparently, she had been talking to me for a while before I noticed. Tad elbowed me in the ribs, and muttered, "Attention, Captain Spedling! All hands on deck!"

See, I have this problem. I get kind of spacey some-times, and I miss some of the things my teachers say. That happens to a lot of kids who have had leuke-mia, because the chemotherapy drugs and radiation can mess up your brain permanently. Some kids come through it totally fine, but I'm not one of those kids. I never even had radiation, but I did have "high-dose and intrathecal methotrexate," which is the fancy way of saying that the doctors used to shoot poison into my spinal cord and bathe my brain in it. And it left me a little scrambled up. By the way, Tad used to make fun of other kids' disabilities all the time. I didn't really like it, but trying to make Tad politically correct was just a recipe for disaster.

"Uh, sorry, Miss Palma," I said. "I was just really concentrating on my writing."

She smiled sweetly. "That's funny, Jeffrey. You know, I taught your older brother, Steven. He was exactly the same way."

"Spastic?" Tad whispered, not very quietly.

She gave him a look. "Thoughtful," she said.

Wow, this was new. Teachers never had any

patience for my learning problems. And they definitely never told me I was anything like my perfect older brother. The bell rang then, and Miss Palma smiled again. "Well, class," she said over the sound of twenty-seven kids unzipping their backpacks, "I can't wait to see how we learn and grow together this year." It was the kind of dorky thing that teachers say all the time, but I had the feeling Miss Palma really meant what she said. That's when I started to think that maybe eighth grade could be different from all of the other horrible school years I'd had.

As Tad would say, "Hoping is your first mistake."

HOT LEGS

That first week of school had at least one other huge highlight: I met the girl of my dreams. I mean, it's not like we had some exclusive relationship or anything. She was probably the girl of just about everyone's dreams. But I'm the guy who made friends with her first.

Kind of.

It happened just before science class, first thing in the morning on the first day of school. I was trying to hustle through the crowded chaos of the hallway, which is hard to do with a limp. As I came around a corner, I saw a girl crouched down on the floor, attempting to gather up a million papers, along with the contents of her entire backpack. People were stepping around her, and even right over her stuff, but nobody was stopping to help. I figured I'd be late to class if I stopped, but I also figured this girl was going to get stampeded if someone didn't help her to pick up her stuff before the warning bell rang.

I knelt next to her and started grabbing lipsticks, packs of gum, and — uh — feminine items. Her dark hair totally covered her face, so I didn't get a look at her until we had gotten everything back together and stood up. When she looked sideways at me to say thank you, I felt my entire world shift violently on its axis. I'd heard people say that beauty can hit you suddenly, but I had thought it was a figure of speech. Uh-uh. This was like, *Ka-POW!*

Miss Ka-POW! spoke, and the torrent of words was as overwhelming as her looks. "Hey, thanks! Wow, people around here are really serious about getting to class on time. Back in California, nobody would have helped a new kid, either, but that's because they'd be worried about not looking cool. But here — geez! I felt like I was, like, in the middle of a riot. Hi, I'm Lindsey. Lindsey Abraham. We just moved here from L.A. Well, not really L.A. The O.C., technically. But close enough, right? And you're . . . ?"

I was speechless. The neurologist would tell you I have "slow processing as a late effect," which is another way of saying that people can really make me look dumb if they're quick talkers. And apparently Lindsey Abraham was, like, an intercontinental talking missile. By the time my brain worked its way through her whole train of thought, I must have looked like a total goon. "Uh, it's Jeffrey. Jeffrey Alper. From New Jersey." *Oh, good God*, I thought. *Did I really just say that?*

She giggled. "Well, hello, Jeffrey Alper from New Jersey. And thanks again for being the one person who stopped to help." The bell rang. "Ooh, now I've made you late to class."

"It's OK, my class is right here. I hope you don't think our whole school is rude. Someone would have stopped to help, but, you know, first day and all. . . ."

Lindsey Abraham smiled at me. Wow, do people have white teeth in California, or what? "It's all right. Someone *did* stop to help. By the way, are you one of those people who always see the good in everybody?"

"I try."

We looked at each other, and for that instant, we were equal — I don't think she knew what to say, either. Of course, she recovered first. "You said your class is this one, right?" She squinted at her schedule, which was partly crumpled in her hand and had a big sneaker footprint across it. "Science with, uh, Laurenzano?"

"Yeah, but watch out going in. He's famous for getting mad when people come in late."

Lindsey smiled again. *I could get used to that smile*, I thought. On second thought, no, I'd probably never get used to it. I liked it, though. A lot. "Come with me," she said. "I owe you one. Is that the back door of this room? OK, you hit that one, and I'll go in the front." Then she turned on her heel and barged into the room like it was a Hollywood party and she was on the red carpet. I headed for the back door. What else was I going to do?

Miraculously, Mr. Laurenzano was nowhere in sight. Kids were grabbing seats for their friends, but there was still a totally empty table for four at the back of the room, so I kind of eased my way over there, hoping nobody would notice I was late. I sat in one chair, and pulled the chair next to mine away to save a space for Tad.

Meanwhile, in front of the room, Lindsey was the star attraction. It was like a movie scene or something: Everybody's conversations just totally stopped as she walked across the floor. Nobody was going to notice me *now*. She smiled at the closest guy — this chess geek named Connor — and said, "Is this Mr. Laurenzano's room?" He just swallowed a few times, then nodded. "Thanks," she said. "I'm new here, and this school is *so* confusing! At my old school in California, we didn't have all these inside hallways. It was more like —"

Mr. Laurenzano popped out of the little back room that lab classrooms always have, and said, "Seats, everybody! We have science to do!" Lindsey looked around for an empty place, and my table was her only option. I couldn't believe my luck. She glided over, gestured toward the chair directly across from me, and raised one eyebrow. "Be my guest," I said.

Wow, was that a slick line, or what? "Be my guest." So suave, so smooth. This girl's heart would be mine by third period.

As if.

Lindsey sat down, and the smell of her perfume wafted across to me. I was hypnotized. Mr. Laurenzano started taking attendance, and when he got to her name, I repeated it in my mind: *Lindsey Abraham*. Such a perfect name: five syllables that rolled right across the tongue. Lindsey Abraham. I wondered how much it would hurt to get those fourteen letters tattooed on my arm.

Unfortunately, I realized, if somebody wanted to get all of that onto my bicep, they would have to write pretty small. But maybe just the initials? L.A. And she was from there, too! It was perfect. Now if only I didn't —

"Jeffrey Alper!" Mr. Laurenzano was calling my name, his lower lip already curling into a sneer of distaste. And everybody was staring at me, including Lindsey. Apparently, this wasn't the first time he'd said it. But this wasn't my usual spacing-out problem. This was, like, a hormonal emergency. Lindsey grinned.

I thought I might pass out.

"Here," I said weakly.

"Mr. Alper, I don't know what kind of attention your seventh-grade science teacher demanded, but in this classroom, you will be silent and attentive at all times. We will be working with dangerous, flammable —"

Lindsey was grinning at me. Her lips were lush and perfect, sparkling and glossy. I just wanted to stare at them until —

"Is that understood, Mr. Alper?"

"Uh, absolutely," I replied automatically. I mean, I had no clue what I was supposed to have understood, but I didn't think asking this guy to repeat himself would help. Just then, the classroom door opened, and Tad wheeled himself over to my table. He looked at me, then at Lindsey, who had stopped grinning, and was looking coolly at him. Then he looked back at me, and kind of smirked down into his book bag as he took out his laptop computer. Tad and I are allowed to type everything. A lot of cancer survivors do fine in school, but Tad and I both have tons of nerve damage, so we get special accommodations — as Tad says, we're kind of like honorary speds. Both of us have really horrendous handwriting because our hands aren't very coordinated, so voilà! We get laptops.

Other kids are always jealous of our laptop privileges, and once in a while someone mutters something about it. When we were in seventh grade, this one kid named Tim said it wasn't fair, and Tad just about lost his mind right in the middle of social studies. He was all, like, "Not fair? Oh, I'm sorry I get this lovely laptop computing device when all you get is the ability to walk, control your hands, and know you'll probably survive until your eighteenth birthday." Then the kid was going, "Uh, I didn't mean . . ." But Tad wasn't done yet. While the whole class watched in horror, he put his hands through the metal support braces on the arms of his wheelchair and forced himself to stand up. Then he took a shaky little step to the side, gestured toward the chair, and said, "Why don't you take a turn with the laptop? You can even have my seat."

The teacher was totally pale and panicked. She said, "Um, Tad, why don't you just . . . I'm sure Timothy wasn't trying to . . . uh . . ." Tim looked like he wanted to die on the spot, but Tad still wasn't finished. He said, "What, Timmy? Don't you want to trade places anymore? Then you could be a partial cripple instead of a . . ." At that point, Tad had to stop and catch his breath because it's really hard for him to support himself. I rushed around a couple of desks to get to Tad, and tried to help him back into his seat. This brought on one of his alarming coughing fits, but as he sank back down into his chair, I'm pretty sure everyone in the room noticed that a couple of the coughs were really the end of his sentence: ". . . complete COUGHing COUGHhead."

I knew he had it ten times worse than I did with the late effects, and I knew a lot of people didn't like the way he never, ever held anything back, but at moments like that I always wished I could be even a tenth as brave as Tad.

OK, so now you know the deal with the laptops. Anyway, Tad got his booted up, and then just as Mr. Laurenzano launched into part two of his amazing lab safety speech, my computer pinged. Lindsey looked for a moment, but then went back to staring out the window. Apparently she wasn't a huge lab safety fan. Mr. Laurenzano gave me a warning glare, but didn't come over from behind the big old slate-topped demonstration table in front of the room. Science teachers never come out from behind the big table. I looked down at my screen, and saw that Tad had IM'ed me:

Tadditude:	Wow, Jeff, who's the babe?
Dangerous_pie:	Your mom.
Tadditude:	No, the one three feet away from you.
Dangerous_pie:	Oh, that's Lindsey Abraham. I had her flown in from California for my personal amusement. You

	can look at her if you want, though.
Tadditude:	Sweet. But have you talked to her yet?
Dangerous_pie:	Uh-huh. We're really close.
Tadditude:	Intro me?
Dangerous_pie:	After class.
Tadditude:	Duh.

Just then, I noticed that a large shadow had fallen over my screen. I couldn't even bear to look up as Mr. Laurenzano said, "Thaddeus Ibsen, Lindsey Abraham. Lindsey, Thaddeus. There, you've been introduced. NOW can I teach some science?"

Wow, it looked like this was going to be my year for unusual teachers.

For the rest of the period, I totally tried to concentrate, but it was impossible. I kept thinking about how Lindsey's legs were just inches from mine under the table. And I know that's totally inappropriate, and you probably think I'm some kind of sick perverted horndog, but hey, it's the truth. During our brief but meaningful forty-minute relationship, I had noted that: A. Lindsey was wearing a skirt, and B. She had hot legs.

Even if I could have torn my brain away from the new love of my life, it wasn't like I could have ignored the distraction of Tad. I had turned off the sound on my computer, but he was still IM'ing me nonstop. I kept whispering for him to cut it out, but he's not very, um, directable. And every time I looked at him, he rolled his eyes from me to Lindsey and back, over and over again. It looked like he was having some kind of spasm. Fortunately, Lindsey didn't notice, because she had turned halfway around in her chair to face Mr. Laurenzano.

Which allowed me to add the back of her neck to my list of perfect things about Lindsey Abraham.

After about a million years, the warning bell rang, and Tad wheeled himself out. He always got to go either at the warning bell, or three minutes after everybody else, because it was hard for him to get through the halls if they were full of people. When the rest of us got dismissed, Lindsey looked right at me and said, "Um, Jeff?"

Wow, she remembered my name. Unfortunately, she was probably so mortified by Tad that she would never speak to either of us again. "Yeah?"

"What was that about?"

"What was *what* about?" If this girl didn't think I was a complete moron yet, she had to be getting pretty close.

"You know, why did the teacher introduce me to your friend Thad?"

"It's Tad. And he introduced you because, uh . . . well . . ." Here's where a smarter guy would have just shut up. But for some reason, whenever I'm under pressure, I have this awful habit of telling the truth. "We were IM'ing about you." I could feel a brilliant crimson blush spreading across my cheeks as Lindsey cocked her head to the side and chewed on a lock of her gorgeous hair.

"Oh." She broke into a grin. "Were you saying anything good?"

Now the blush was hitting my neck. My ears felt red-hot, too, and I was sweating. "No!"

"No? You mean, you were saying something bad? That's not nice!" She wagged her finger back and forth at me like preschool teachers do when they want to show a kid that pegging teachers with the blocks is a no-no. But the grin was still there.

"NO! We weren't saying anything bad about you, either. We were just, uh . . . I mean, I think you're nice. That's all."

She giggled a little. "You just told Tag that you think I'm nice, huh? I'm so sure!"

"For real! And it's Thad. I mean, Tad." That was it. She had to think I had the approximate IQ of lettuce by this point. Before I could dig myself any deeper into the Pit of Conversational Stupidity, the late bell rang.

"See what you did, Jeff? First you go writing about me all over town, and now you made me late to class again. Well, there's only one thing to do."

"What?"

"Walk me to my next class. That way, I can use

the new-student excuse, and you can be my new-student escort. Nobody ever gets marked late if they're showing the new girl around." She grabbed her stuff and headed out the door. I was still kind of paralyzed by this whole conversation. Partly, it was the slow-processing thing. But mostly, it was the Lindsey Effect.

When she hit the hall, Lindsey turned to me and said, "Come *on*, Jeff! Unless you think a more IM-worthy *babe* is going to stroll along any minute." As I scrambled to catch up to her without tripping over my weak right foot, she punched me in the arm. "By the way," she said, "there are two things you really ought to know. First of all, classroom windows are very reflective. If you're not careful, someone sitting across from you might be able to look at them and read your computer screen."

Oh, geez. "What's the other thing?"

"You're cute when you blush."

Sometimes it's hard to know whether I should curl up in a ball and die of embarrassment, or give myself a hearty high five.

LOST IN THE MAIL

That day when I got home and saw the mail, I did something really stupid. I mean, ultra-intensely, radioactively idiotic. But before I tell you what it was, I have to tell you a little bit about my dad and me. And math. Otherwise, you won't understand WHY I did it.

First of all, you should know that my dad is an accountant. He loves numbers. I mean, when we go to a minor-league Yankees game at this stadium near our house, Dad always buys a program. So far, that's not so weird, right? You're probably thinking, *What's the big deal? My dad always buys the program at games, too.* But my dad always, always fills out the scorecard for the game as it goes along. He never leaves his seat or misses a play, because then he might not get every single bit of info on the card perfectly. I know, I know. Your dad keeps score, too, right? But my dad prints out every player's stats at home before the game and brings them with him, along with a pen. Then, as the game goes along, he recomputes each player's stats in real time. So if a player is batting .317 after a hundred and forty at bats, and then strikes out, my dad will be sitting there, filling out his card at top speed while mumbling, *"a hundred and forty-one at bats now, with an additional out . . . carry the three . . . HEY, JEFFREY, FEENEY'S AVERAGE JUST DROPPED TO THREE-SIXTEEN! Well, actually, three-fifteen point eight three repeating, but . . ."* Usually, that's when I go get some peanuts and Cracker Jacks. And unlike my father, I don't care if I never get back.

As for me, I don't love math. In fact, I am tremendously awful at it. The trouble started when I was in fourth grade, which was my first full year back in school after my cancer treatment ended. My teacher started noticing that I didn't pay attention, that I lost my homework sheets pretty often, and that I didn't know my math facts. Now, the weird thing is that when I was little, my dad used to call me his little math expert. I knew all of my addition and subtraction stuff before kindergarten.

And then I didn't know it anymore. Blame it on the methotrexate, I guess. The doctors did. The social workers and child life specialists at the hospital did. My mother did. But Dad blamed me. I remember he made me about a million different kinds of flash cards. There were flash cards with little pictures. Flash cards cut into different shapes. Different-size ones. Color-coded ones. But nothing ever really helped. A lot of times, he'd make me prove I totally knew my stuff before he'd let me go to bed. Then in the morning, he'd ruffle my hair and send me off to school to take a math test. When the test would hit my desk, I'd realize — BAM! — the facts were all gone from my head.

Dad worked with me all through that year, but I could tell he was getting madder and madder at me. Then in fifth grade, even though nobody said anything to me about it, all of a sudden my mom and Steven took over as my homework helpers. Dad just sat in the living room and complained about my grades, my wandering attention, and my lack of effort. Whenever I brought home a test, he'd say,

"Why don't you just try a little harder, Jeffrey?" Mom would try to shush him, but it never quite worked.

He never understood that I *was* trying. To this day, I don't think he can comprehend that a child of his could just totally bite at math. But I do. No matter how hard I concentrate, or how many hours I spend trying to memorize facts and patterns, whenever the test comes along, everything starts swimming around in my head until I'm drowning in an evil math whirlpool.

Now back to the letter. It was in the mail when I got home, addressed from the superintendent of the school district to the PARENTS OF JEFFREY ALPER, GRADE EIGHT. Both of my parents were at work, and Steven was already wandering around Africa with a pair of bongos strapped to his back, so there was nobody to stop me from opening the letter. I couldn't figure out what I had done to get in trouble so early in the year, but you can believe I was dying to know. I debated for about twelve seconds, but of course I gave in and ripped that sucker open like a raging rodeo bull going after a slow cowboy. I mean, I'd never gotten a letter from the superintendent before.

I should have waited. It was a boring letter anyway, with all these super-awkward phrases like "educational equity" and "assessment regime" and "holistic integrity of the K-12 system." Plus, it wasn't just for my parents. Every family in the district got a copy. And truthfully, it took me about five tries before I could even understand what the guy was saying: That from now on, no kid could get promoted from grade four, eight, or eleven unless he passed the huge, horrifying state standardized tests in April.

I was screwed. I knew my dad would have a cow, and that as soon as he saw it, he'd start pushing math on me so hard that every time I sneezed, fractions would fly out of my nose. Fortunately for me, my father never thinks to look for the mail by taking apart the garbage disposal, so that's where the letter went.

When my parents got home, I didn't say anything

about the letter. There was a lot to talk about any-way, because of course my mom wanted to know every detail in the world about my teachers, my schedule, and my "classmates." I swear, she actually used the word "classmates." It scares me sometimes when I stop to consider the fact that she's a high school teacher. Thankfully, she teaches over the border in Pennsylvania, so we don't have to run into her students wherever we go. I don't think I'd be able to stand the embarrassment of listening to her using her corny lingo on them.

As you might imagine, I didn't tell her about my beloved new classmate. I did mention Miss Palma, though, and Mom got all misty-eyed: "Oh, honey! Your brother loved her! I just know you will, too. And he wrote the most wonderful journals in her class."

"Really?" I hadn't heard about this. "What were they about?"

My parents exchanged a Significant Glance Across the Table. Aha! Apparently, Steven's journals had been about me. "Well," Dad said, "Steven had a difficult eighth-grade year. That was the year we found out about your . . ."

He stopped midsentence. Even now, he just can't bring himself to say the word. "My cancer, Dad?"

He nodded.

Mom said, "I wonder what ever happened to Steven's old journal. It might be interesting for you to go back and see what your brother was thinking when he was your age. Hmm . . . that was the year he and Annette got close. And before that, he had the biggest, sweetest crush on Renee Albert. You know, from around the corner?"

Oh, I remembered Renee Albert. She was so pretty that I even knew it when I was a little kid. But it was incredibly weird to picture my brother liking anyone but Annette. I mean, up until the summer before my eighth-grade year, Steven and Annette had been, like, eternal soul mates or something. But that was before Steven flipped out, dropped out, and headed off to Africa.

Well, whatever. It would be pretty interesting to see Steven's journals from back then, but it's not like

I was going to start digging for them in his room, or the Steven Alper Slept Here Shrine, as I call it. I supposed I could have asked him for permission, if he even still had them, but he was only checking e-mail once every couple of weeks in Africa. Apparently, he was spending most of his time at an old safari camp outside of Nairobi, where drummers from all over the world come to teach one another their native rhythms.

Long story.

After the dinner/interrogation, I needed to get out of the house. I told my parents I was going out for some physical therapy, and headed for the garage. See, thanks to a drug called vincristine, I have nerve damage in my right foot that makes it drag when I try to lift it. If you're sitting in a chair as you read this, put your right foot flat on the floor. Now, without lifting the rest of your leg, lift the front of your foot up so your toes are off the ground.

Congratulations. You just did something I will never, ever do again.

That makes running, jumping, even walking, pretty hard. But because of some other cancer complications, I tend to turn into a fat whale if I don't exercise a ton. It's bad enough that I'm a short kid with big, round glasses — the last thing I need is to get porked out again like I used to be back in sixth grade, when Tad announced that I looked like a cross between Ben Franklin and a Franklin stove. So it's crucial for me to stay in shape. That's why I have a hobby: I ride my bike, like, sixty miles a week all summer. During the school year, when I'm excused from all team sports in gym, I ride the exercise bike instead. And every May for the last few years, I've pedaled twenty-five miles in The Moving On Bike-a-Thon, a bike ride for cancer survivors, to raise money for leukemia research and treatment.

I can't walk too well, but when I'm on my bike, I can fly.

Five minutes later, I was zooming down a long, long hill to the edge of the Delaware River where there's a bike path that runs for miles and miles. I love going downhill so fast that I can feel the wind vibrating against my helmet, although believe it or not, my favorite thing is going up a long hill. Anybody can fly down a hill, but it takes a serious bike guy to fly *up* a hill.

I'm a serious bike guy.

My mind wanders when I ride, and that day it wandered out over the oceans until it reached my big brother. Steven had always been my hero. He was like the rock that the rest of my life leaned on. During my cancer treatment, he used to make me laugh when nobody else could, and he was the one person who had never, ever cried in front of me about my cancer.

The only time I can ever remember Steven crying over any of it was after my treatment, when I tried to use my foot on his bass drum pedal, and we realized I could never play a drum set.

Anyway, after my treatment ended, Steven was still the person who kept me calm. The beginning of third grade was the first time I was healthy enough to attend the first day of a school year since kindergarten, and I was totally nervous about it. I didn't know whether any of my friends would be in my class, or what the teacher would be like. I prayed she would be patient with me when I didn't know something everyone else had learned already, or when I spaced out. Plus, I always worried about recess: Would anybody pick me for their team even though I couldn't really run or catch? If not, would any other boy be doing anything besides playing ball? Or — worst-case scenario — would I have to hang out with the *girls*? So when I woke up scared in the middle of the night, Steven heard me and followed me downstairs to the kitchen. Even though it was the night before the first day of his junior year of high school — and Dad had probably told him a billion times that *junior year is the year the colleges really look at* — Steven stayed up and listened to me cry and whine.

When I was all worried out, Steven picked me up and carried me back to bed. He even tucked me in, and before he left my room, he whispered, "If they don't let you be on a team, tell me. I'll drive over there and kick their little third-grader butts."

My last thought before sleep was a picture of my big brother crashing his car through the playground fence, jumping out, and chasing all the kids who got picked before me up a tree.

By the time Steven left for New York University two years after that, he was my tutoring lifeline, too. I freaked out in his room while he was packing, and he swore to me that I could text him or send an e-mail anytime I needed to. So even when he was in another state, I never felt like he was *really* gone.

Then all of a sudden last spring he had some kind of meltdown in the middle of wrapping up his third year of college, and decided to take a leave of absence from school. And from Annette. And from pretty much all contact with me — I mean, when he told us he wouldn't have e-mail or cell phone access in Africa, I felt like I'd been smacked with a two-by-four. Was I shocked? Oh, yeah.

Remember a few years ago, when scientists announced that Pluto wasn't a planet anymore? All of a sudden, that was the main story in the news for, like, a week and a half. I remember being all worried for some reason I could never name, and I think that happened to a lot of people. It's not like the planet-hood status of Pluto was a major factor in anybody's conscious life before that, but when Pluto suddenly stopped being a planet, the whole world was unnerved. Like, if they can take away Pluto, *what's next?* What if the sun isn't — *a sun?* What if I'm really adopted? What if everyone in my town was secretly whisked away in the middle of the night and *replaced by exact replica aliens?*

OK, you can see why creative writing is my only good subject. But my point is, Steven's relationship with Annette — and with me and Mom and Dad — was like Pluto being a planet. Until it wasn't. One day in May, Steven showed up at home unexpectedly and announced to my parents that he was finished with school. He had to go out into the world and find himself. And he needed to do it — *alone.*

Basically, my hero woke up one day and quit the world.

THE PACT

The next day in school, everybody was totally going insane over the letters. The math teacher lectured us about how this proved the seriousness of her subject, and how we had to *buckle down* and apply ourselves. I mean, what does that even mean? Are we supposed to strap ourselves to our desks? Tighten our pants a notch? Put on straitjackets?

In social studies, the teacher lectured us for forty minutes on the history of aptitude testing, and how the Nazis tried to use IQ tests to prove their insane racist theories. Maybe this was just a hunch, but I had a feeling she wasn't a big fan of the new rule.

Mr. Laurenzano gave us a whole spiel about how just because science wasn't on the state test, that didn't mean it wasn't an important subject. Plus, he said, we'd be using tons of math and reading skills in our science work, so obviously we should pay careful attention in his class every single instant. At least, I think that's what he said, but I wasn't paying such careful attention. Mostly I was just trying to turn my computer screen at an angle so Lindsey couldn't read Tad's completely inappropriate IMs in the window.

Miss Palma discussed the new rule, then outlined the reading and writing portions of the test. You know, in case some kid had just moved to New Jersey from Mongolia. Or California, come to think of it. When she was all done with that, some girl raised her hand and asked whether the rule would change what we would be learning for the year. Miss Palma's nostrils flared and she said, "I have always taught my students to read well and write well. Now, why in the world would I let some idiotic *test* interfere with that?" She turned to the chalkboard and pressed the chalk so hard it squeaked as she wrote the day's journal topic: Write about a time you were pressured to do something with which you didn't agree.

All righty, then.

In gym, I thought for sure we would be safe from the test lecture. I was wrong. There are five gym teachers in my school, four of whom are sane. The fifth, Mr. McGrath, was in charge of my class. I'd never had him as a teacher before, but I knew him because he sometimes came into the workout room and yelled randomly during other gym teachers' classes. He liked to scream and yell, and he had this odd habit of emphasizing random syllables. When we got there, we dressed in our ultra-dorky two-tone green gym uniforms, and then he made everyone sit on these red dots on the floor, in order of our last names.

That put me, Jeffrey Alper, right behind Lindsey Abraham. Believe me, I had never before loved the concept of alphabetical order so deeply. Amazingly, despite the fact that I looked very much like an ear of corn in my uniform, Lindsey looked like a stunning supermodel in hers. I could barely stand to look at her. But that didn't stop me.

Once everyone was on the right dot, Mr. McGrath

shouted at us for about fifteen minutes about how all this testing was a bad idea. I was with him there, but then he started in on how all the brainpower in the world wasn't as important as staying in shape. It was like he thought we were marines, and he was our drill sergeant:

"We were all born with two things: a body, and a brain. The *prob*-lem is that you all sit in school all day on your big, old, cushy *hi*-neys working on the brain part. Then you go home, and what do you do? You sit around some more. And let me tell you, when I was a kid, we didn't have any of this Nintendo, Sega Genesis, Wii, three-D GameCube stuff. Our three-D game platform was called a *park*. Our Nin-*ten*-do virtual reality war game was called hide-and-seek. And *Wii* was the sound we made when we jumped fifteen feet from a tire swing."

It seemed to me like maybe Mr. McGrath had taken a couple of headers off of that tire swing. But he wasn't done yet.

"So that's why we will be de-*vo*-ting this year to getting your gigantic, soft pos-*tee*-riors into tip-top condition. We're gonna run. And when I say 'run' I mean, 'RUN.'"

Lindsey suddenly turned to me and said, "Aha. I always wondered what people meant when they said 'run.'" I laughed. How could someone with such a perfect neck be so funny, too? Somewhere in the world, there had to be an eighth-grade girl with no neck who still told knock-knock jokes and wondered why the world was so cruel.

Mr. McGrath was reaching a climax. "We're gonna *lift*. We're gonna work out. That's what I did every day when I was your age, and that's what *earned* me the citywide two hundred–meter running title in nineteen eighty-one and nineteen eighty-two. That's what *earned* me my high school nickname: *Flash* McGrath. And that's what will get you into the best physical condition of your lives. And I know you won't be thanking me now. But you'll be thanking me *la*-ter, when you get married and your wedding dress doesn't have to be the size of a *pup tent* to fit over your massive, rounded —"

"Wow," Lindsey said. "One day, I *will* have to come

back and thank him for his touching interest in the shape and well-being of my butt. What do you think?"

I thought if Lindsey mentioned her butt again I would have a heart attack. She turned back around and I tried to compose myself as I watched my red-faced lunatic of a gym teacher finish his rant. He was so out of breath he had to stop to rest and wipe his face on a little towel he kept hanging from the back pocket of his sweatpants. His huge sweatpants.

It was pretty ironic, really, but Flash McGrath weighed about three hundred pounds and smoked like a chimney. I looked across the gym to where Tad was sitting in his wheelchair. He reached back, patted his butt, and raised one eyebrow. I laughed. But I also wondered what was going to happen if the obese fitness nut and Tad started getting on each other's nerves. When Tad decided he didn't like a teacher, the results weren't always pretty.

Halfway through the period, Mr. McGrath ordered the class to do a bunch of push-ups, sit-ups, and jumping jacks. I mumbled something to Lindsey about having to go somewhere, left my dot, and walked over to the glassed-in side room where they keep the state-of-the-art exercise bikes, treadmills, stair climbers, elliptical machines, and weight training equipment. Normally that stuff is just for the athletic teams, but ever since Tad and I had been put on a physical therapy plan in sixth grade, we got to go in there, too. Tad was supposed to walk on the treadmill for a few minutes every day to strengthen his muscles and bones, and I was allowed to use whichever machines I wanted as long as I got my heart rate up.

On a usual day, I worked until the sweat poured out, while Tad sat in his chair and made wisecracks. I got onto the exercise bike and started pedaling, and Tad popped a wad of gum in his mouth. He began blowing bubbles and chatting with me as though I wasn't in the middle of a workout.

"So, D.A., did your parents (POP!) freak over the letter?" He calls me D.A. sometimes. The *D* stands for "Dumb."

"No. Why would they freak?"

"Uh, because you always totally bomb the state test, and your parents (POP!) probably want you to make it out of middle school before they croak of old age."

"Thanks for the vote of confidence, Tad. It means a lot to me."

"No (POP!) problem. I've got your back. Speaking of which, what are we going to (POP!) do about the test?"

"What do you mean? We're going to take it. It will be fine. Plus, it's, like, eight months away. Why are we even talking about this *now*?"

"Because I am not (POP!) going to high school without you. You might be a D.A., but you're *my* D.A."

"Dude. Dude. It's all good. I'm going to high school. Now will you be quiet and let me work out?"

"Fine. I bet Lindsey Abraham will miss you next year, though."

I stopped pedaling. "All right, genius. What's the plan?"

"Simple. I tutor you."

"How's that going to help? You tutor me now half the time."

"No, I mean, I *seriously* tutor you. Hours and hours, one (POP!) on one. It'll be kind of fun, hanging out with your pal Tad and doing lots of good old math. But I'm warning you — I'm gonna *work* that chemo-soaked little brain of yours. Think of how much you'll learn (POP!). You might be a math-tard now, but by April, I'll turn you into a fire-breathing math machine. You'll eat, breathe, and sleep math problems. Buddy, by the time I'm done with you, you'll (POP!) *be* a math problem. We're gonna —"

"No."

"What did you say?"

"No. Why bother? I'm never going to pass anyway."

"What are you talking about, Jeff? You have to (POP!) pass this thing, man. You *have* to."

Tad has never understood how much I hate math. I guess he's similar to my father that way. It's like they're both fish, and they think I'm a moron because no matter how much they pressure me, I don't suddenly start breathing water. But it's not my fault that the chemo messed up my math skills and left Tad's alone. "Tad, I can't pass it. I don't just hate math. I really, really suck at it. You might as well tutor a tree."

"D.A., I'm not going to let you give up on this. There's no option."

"Sure there is. I could just, uh . . ."

"All right, fine. I don't have to start tutoring you right away (POP!). Your parents could try to get you exempted from the testing requirement. Maybe if the school puts it in your five-oh-four plan or something."

A 504 plan is what you get if you've got problems that mess with your learning, but your parents or the school don't want to put you in special ed. Tad calls it "Sped Lite."

Tad kept talking. It's pretty hard to stop him once he gets going. And he's *always* going. "Why don't you just go home and ask your parents to start working on this? Your mom's a teacher — I bet she knows all the angles. And your dad could —"

"I said NO!!!"

Tad was so startled he actually rolled backward a step or two. I never stand up to him. He thought for a few seconds. When he spoke again, I could hear the amazement in his voice. "Oh, geez. Your parents didn't *get* the letter, did they?"

I looked away.

"*Did* they?"

"Not so much," I mumbled.

"Holy cow, D.A. This is bad. This is very bad. What were you *thinking?*"

I didn't reply. But that never stops the Tadmeister. "OK, you weren't thinking. No problem, then. We'll just go back to Plan A."

I couldn't help myself. "What the heck is Plan A?"

"Tutoring time. Your parents don't need to know a thing."

I buried my head in my hands. "You still don't get it. I won't pass this test no matter *what* you do. It would be like . . . like telling *you* that you couldn't graduate unless you walk across the stage to get your diploma. It's not tricky. It's not hard. It's

48

not a little problem for you to solve. It...is...
impossible!"

"I could walk across the stage if I wanted to. I just
don't want to."

"Tad, that's not the point. This isn't about you.
The point is . . ."

Tad wheeled right up next to my bike. He looked
pretty mad. "It is about me, you stupid little . . ." He
stopped and breathed hard for a little while. "Look,
everyone's always assuming we can't do things. *Oh,
Thaddeus, you're too sickly to be in gym. But it's OK.
You're too weak to use your own damn hand to write.
But don't worry about it.* Don't you see? Even if nobody
else thinks so, you can pass this test, Jeff. You can.
And I can —"

"You can what? Get all the glory for saving your
semi-moronic friend?"

"No, Jeff. I can walk across the stage at graduation. All right? That's the deal. We're a team. I tutor
you, and you work out with me. You pass, I walk."

"You're serious?"

"As cancer."

I didn't want to do this. I just wanted to close my eyes and hope it all went away. But I heard a rustle next to me, and suddenly Tad was standing up. He took a step and put his hand on my shoulder.

"Come on," he said. "How hard can it be?"

THE HANDSOME BABE MAGNET
RIDES AGAIN

When I got home that afternoon, I was starving. I decided to make some oatmeal. That's kind of my tradition when I'm uptight about something. I guess there are worse things I could do under stress, right?

Some kids do drugs. Some kids light stuff on fire. Me, I heat oats. It started when I was a little kid. My parents liked to sleep late, so Steven used to make me oatmeal for breakfast. That was the best — no grown-ups in sight, a hot meal in front of me, and my big brother by my side. Then, when I got a little older, I started making the oatmeal for Steven. I remember the morning after his high school prom, when I was nine, I brought him oatmeal in bed at eight AM. He chased me out of the room by throwing about fifteen pillows and pieces of dirty laundry at me. Then, about five minutes later, he came out to the kitchen and said, "So where's my oatmeal, you little madman?"

I wonder if they have oatmeal in Africa. I bet they

do, but they probably call it "ukumani" or something. And I bet they throw a few really disgusting, many-limbed bugs into the pot for flavor. I kind of hope so.

Anyway, the key to oatmeal, Alper Brothers–style, is your milk-to-water ratio. It's got to be a fifty-fifty mixture. Once you've got that down, you can basically chuck anything in there as long as it's sweet. Myself, I'm big on berries. Or honey and nuts. Steven once made a batch with flaming bananas on top, but I'm not that brave.

Plus, sometimes my hands shake, so the flame part could get ugly.

On this day, I had my water and milk going on the stove, my oats standing by in a measuring cup, and a little pack of Craisins mixed with brown sugar ready to be dumped in at the end. As I stirred the liquid, I started thinking about Lindsey Abraham. I had never really liked a girl before. I mean, I had noticed a ton of girls in my life, and I had a lot of female friends. But nobody had ever rocked my whole entire planet out of its orbit in two days before. And she seemed to be flirting with me.

On the other hand, I figured I had no shot with her whatsoever. For one thing, she was probably flirting with everybody. She was at a new school, with no connections, and she was ultra-beautiful, so why wouldn't she be checking out all of her options? And, let's face it, I was nobody's idea of the hottest guy in eighth grade. Here's a partial list of male eighth graders who put me to shame:

- Matt Hanuszak, sports stud
- Dylan Straniere, once appeared in a commercial (even if it *was* for cat food)
- David Nedermayer, lives in mansion, hosts pool parties
- Josh Albert, is nearly as good-looking as his famously hot cousin, Renee
- That one goth kid with the black crosses on his guitar (even though he wears eyeliner)

Even if she were somehow, against all odds, a bit interested in me, I knew that would all change once we had "The Conversation." Every cancer survivor out there has had The Conversation a million times, and it never goes well. You kind of try to hem and haw, to put it off, to pretend you don't limp everywhere and carry a laptop to all of your classes, but ultimately, anyone who might become friendly with you must find out about your cancer history. And people say the stupidest crap in the world to you right after it comes out. Here are three possibilities, drawn from my worst experiences:

Me: Well, you see, I, uh, I'm a cancer survivor.

Person #1: And how's that working out for you?

Me: Well, you see, I, uh, I used to have leukemia.

Person #2: Dude, how come you're not, like, *bald*?

Me: Well, you see, I, uh, I had acute lymphocytic lymphoma when I was five.

Person #3:   Whoa. *That* must'a sucked. I
once had my tonsils out. . . .

So how in the world was I ever supposed to get
a girlfriend? There's enough that can go wrong in a
normal boy-girl interaction without throwing in all of
my baggage. But if a regular, ordinary relationship
is like juggling a bunch of different-size, jagged
pieces of metal — and from what had been going on
between my brother and Annette, that seemed to
be a pretty good simile — then throwing cancer
into the mix is like juggling a bunch of different-size,
jagged pieces of metal while riding a skateboard on
the edge of the Grand Canyon.

I mean, Lindsey Abraham could have her pick of
any guy she wanted. So why would she choose me?

But, I thought, *she was totally joking around with me
in gym. About her butt.*

Don't get your hopes up.

But she was.

*But you're a short, chubby kid with glasses, a limp, and
brain damage.*

And your oatmeal is boiling over.

By the time my parents came home, I had managed to scrub about 80 percent of the burned, milky goo off of the burner. Mom made pasta for dinner, and the garlic scent mostly covered up the lingering odor of my disaster. As we sat down to eat, Dad wanted to know all about my academic subjects, as usual. But Mom had other ideas:

"Jeffrey, who's this Lindsey girl?"

I nearly choked on a chunk of bread, but managed to say, "Whu-huh?" Thankfully, my windpipe cleared from the force of the huge coughing fit that followed, because it would be pretty embarrassing to have "Whu-huh?" as my last words.

"Oh, Jeffrey, I just ran into Mrs. Ibsen at the market. She told me all about your new friend. Tad said she's a glamorous new girl who's swept you off your feet." Mom put her elbows on the table, and leaned all the way toward me. "So what's the deal?"

On second thought, maybe I should have just choked. I looked away from her, and caught Dad's eye. If there's one thing my father gets, it's how to avoid difficult topics. "Wow," he said. "Honey, this sauce is dee-*li*-cious! What do you call it?"

Mom rolled her eyes. "Ragú. Now tell us about Lindsey, Jeffy."

So much for Dad's change-the-subject ploy. "Uh, she's . . . very nice."

Mom looked happier than I'd seen her in a long time. "Honey, *look*! Our baby has a little girlfriend! And he's blushing over her. This is just like the time when Renee Albert came over to tutor Steven in math. Do you remember that, Jeffy? You were five, and you kept asking your brother whether he was going to kiss her. I thought he was going to curl up in a ball and die of embarrassment. But then when she got to the house, she had a cold and —"

Yeah, I remembered that one. My immunity was wrecked from the chemo, so Steven didn't let Renee into the house. It is freaking uncanny how every single memory in the world ties back into having cancer.

But at least I didn't have to talk about Lindsey anymore.

I was going to kill Tad the next time I saw him.

"Speaking of tutors, Mrs. Ibsen also told me that Tad is going to be helping you with math this year. I'm so proud of you!"

I gulped. "You are?"

"Yes, for taking the initiative like this. You've always been so passive about school. It's nice to see that you're taking matters into your own hands *before* there's a problem."

Hah! "Uh, thanks, Mom."

Dad looked up from his plate, where he was busily cutting pasta and veggies into little separate piles. It used to drive Steven crazy, but that's just how Dad rolls. Aw, who am I kidding? It kind of makes me want to scream, too. "That's great, Jeff. Very responsible of you."

Holy cow. Getting called "responsible" by my dad is like getting called "intelligent" by Albert Einstein.

"Oh," my mom said, "you'd better finish up your dinner, Jeff."

"Why?"

"Because Mrs. Ibsen is bringing Tad over at six-thirty. We figured there's no time like the present."

Geez, it was the second day of school. How much tutoring could I possibly need after only two math lessons? As I got up to put my plate in the dishwasher, the doorbell rang. Apparently, I was about to find out. I went down to the garage and opened the door; we had a bell installed there just for Tad because the front step is a problem for him. He rolled in, made his way to the desk in our family room, and immediately booted up his computer.

"Uh, some people say hello when they barge into a friend's house."

"Yeah, and some people waste time and fail math. Sit down, young Jedi. It is time to begin your training." Whoa, boy. It was going to be a long year.

As soon as the computer was ready, Tad slid it over to me. To my horror, he was starting me right off with word problems. The more I read, the more horror I felt. Here was the first one:

> Lindsey is on a train that leaves Grand Central Station at noon. Jeffrey is on a bus leaving from Port Authority at 1 PM. They are both going to Love City, 120 miles away. If Lindsey is traveling at 60 miles per hour, and Jeff is moving at 45 miles per hour, how long will she have to wait for him in Love City?

I looked at Tad. "Where did you get this?"

He smirked. "Easy. There's this Web site called Mathlibs. They're just like Mad Libs, but with word problems. I decided if they can do it, I can do it, and boom — here we are. Now get to work!"

By the end of an hour with Tad, I felt like my brain was going to explode in a gooey, slimy spray all over the keyboard. I asked for a break, and he grudgingly granted one, so I went upstairs to get some drinks. When I got back down, I said, "So why are you obsessed with Lindsey Abraham?"

He raised an eyebrow as he set himself up with some milk and an organic fig bar. We're used to some odd snacks; both of our moms seem to believe that if they just keep our lives nontoxic enough, we'll never get sick again. Anyway, when his mouth was as revoltingly full of mush as possible, he said, "Dude, I am not obsessed with Lindsey Abraham. I am the total opposite of obsessed with Lindsey Abraham. If obsessed with Lindsey Abraham were the sun, my feelings for her would be Pluto — so far from obsession that they're not even a planet in the same solar system."

I think Tad and I might be a little bit obsessed with Pluto.

"Aha!" I said. "So you admit your feelings for her revolve around obsession!"

"Uh, that's a rather tortured metaphor."

"You started it."

He sighed. "Jeff, I am not obsessed with Lindsey. You are."

"Am not."

"That's very mature and logical. I'd imagine Lindsey would be highly impressed."

I forced myself to take a deep breath. There have been many, many times in my life when all that stood between me and strangling Tad was one deep breath.

"OK, I think she's attractive, all right? It's not like I'm going to make a move anyway. I don't even know how to make a move. And I don't see why you have to make a whole stupid math workbook about it."

"What if she likes you back?" he asked.

"Then she'll have to wait in line for me behind your mom."

"No, I'm serious."

"She doesn't like me back. Lindsey, I mean. Your mom is totally into me."

"Ha-ha. I think Lindsey might like you. Why not? She was checking you out in gym. I could tell."

"Oh, because you're such an expert. Thanks, Doctor Ruth Dorkheimer."

"Look, Jeff, when you're all the way at the edge of the action, in a wheelchair, you see things."

"Oh, so all of a sudden having bad legs turns you into the Girl Whisperer?"

"No, it's just — everybody is afraid to stare at me, so they try not to look at me at all. While they're not looking at me, I can study them. And believe me, I think you have a shot with Lindsey."

"And this is your business *why?*"

He took a deep breath. Which was odd; that was my job. Tad never stopped to get control of himself. "You know, after my bone marrow transplant, when I was in isolation, I used to wonder about all kinds of stuff. *Am I going to graduate from high school? Am I going to drive a car?*" He looked away from me. "*Will I live long enough to kiss a girl?* But I never thought about whether there was a girl in the world that could ever be interested in kissing me. Now I wonder that."

I was stunned. Tad never opened up like this. "Don't worry, buddy. The next time I go out with your mom, I'll ask whether she has a friend for you."

He threw a number two pencil at me. Then he busted out with a pack of flash cards and started dealing. Apparently it's a bad idea to mock the tutor's mom. Fun, but bad.

PAYBACK

In phys ed a few days later, it was my time to put Tad to work. Just getting dressed in shorts is a chore for him, but he eventually came out onto the floor. I think a couple of kids noticed that he was prepared, for a change, because there was definitely some whispering as he wheeled his way across the gym.

When we went into the workout room, he asked me, "So what's the plan, Jeff? Do I just jump on the treadmill and start running? Or are we doing calisthenics first? I do a mean jumping jack, except for that part where your feet are supposed to leave the floor. OK, it's more like I'm miming along to 'Y.M.C.A.,' but still. . . ."

I stopped him. "Listen, the important thing is that we start you off slowly, with low-impact activities. The key is to build your aerobic capacity, while developing the major muscles in your legs, without exerting too much stress on your joints before they can handle it. Oh, and we have to work on your flexibility. You've probably lost some range of motion."

He raised an eyebrow. "What?" I said. "You think you're the only one who can use a computer? Plus, I talked to Mrs. Roling." She used to be our physical therapist at Children's Hospital, and I knew she was constantly preaching to Tad about the importance of forcing himself to walk. "Anyway, let's begin with a few stretches, then get you on the exercise bike."

We got into position on the canvas mats in the corner, and I tried to get Tad to stretch his hamstrings and quad muscles. Needless to say, he complained. "Dude, this *hurts*! Is it supposed to hurt?"

I gave him my best Dalai Lama smile. "All progress is painful. Now reach for those toes!"

After a little while, Tad declared himself ready for the bike. He looked like he had just swallowed a cockroach, but I guess he thought the bike sounded better than doing more work on the mat. At least until he started pedaling. I had it on the lowest setting, but it had just been so long since he had tried to do anything major with his legs that he got tired super-fast.

By the end of the first minute, Tad was panting, "Can't you turn this thing down? It's brutal."

"Dude, if I made it any easier it would just spin in the breeze like a pinwheel. Keep going for one more minute." Just then, I happened to look up at the big plate-glass window that separated us from the main part of the gym. There were several kids peering in. One of them was Lindsey. Tad looked up and saw, too. He muttered, "Watch this!" Then he started moving his legs faster, and proceeded to pedal a whole extra minute before he leaned forward and hugged his knees until his breathing slowed.

Three minutes of even the lightest possible pedaling was a huge accomplishment for Tad, and I told him so when he finished. "Don't patronize me," he snarled. "Now it's your turn. Let's get you going with some free weights."

"Wait a minute," I said. "What do you mean, my turn? It was my turn when you tutored me in math the other night. That was the deal: You tutor, I train. So why should I —"

He tilted his head toward the big window. "Chicks dig muscles," he replied. "So get over here, you little doughboy. This won't be so bad. I'll even do it with you."

That sounded fair, but I knew Tad had massively strong arms from pushing his wheelchair around. Meanwhile, I had twitchy, chubby little sausage arms. I sighed and picked up the lightest pair of dumbbells for curling. They weighed five pounds each. Tad grabbed a fifteen-pound weight in each hand. He counted me through three sets of twelve repetitions, matching me rep for rep, and by the end my muscles were shaking uncontrollably. Sweat was pouring into my eyes. Tad had recovered completely, and looked like he was out for a casual little wheelchair jaunt in the park.

"Are we done yet?" I gasped.

"Sure," he said. "Except for the push-ups, the sit-ups, the reverse curls, the lat pull-downs. . . ."

I groaned. Tad barked, "Fine, Mister Bird-chest.

Have it your way. You think it's easy for me to work my legs? You think I'm hanging out in this wheelchair because it's some great fashion statement? Go ahead, keep your wussy spaghetti arms. See if I care." Then he zoomed out of the room.

I didn't understand what I had done wrong, but I felt guilty anyway. I did a set each of push-ups and sit-ups, and staggered to the locker room. I hoped Lindsey hadn't been able to read the numbers on my weights.

In English class, Miss Palma told us we would be starting a unit on reading and writing biographies. She told the class that "in order to get us in the biographical frame of mind," we had two journal assignments for the week:

- Write down, as closely as you can remember, a conversation that you have heard.
- Write a letter to a person you admire.

I knew exactly what to do for the first one, and I got started before Miss Palma even finished speaking.

The one conversation that has been rolling over and over in my head all summer is the argument my brother, Steven, had with my parents when he told them about his plan to take a break from college and travel around Africa playing hand drums. I'm not proud to admit this, but I heard every single word by eavesdropping. There's a big, square ventilation pipe that goes from the kitchen right through the corner of my closet, and I discovered a long time ago that if you put your ear against the cold gray metal of the pipe, you can hear whatever anyone is saying down there.

The secret pipe has always served me well — I haven't been surprised by a Christmas present since I was seven years old — but on this night I shouldn't have listened. At the peak of the argument, my mom said, "Steven, you're being ridiculous. Don't you know that there are people counting on you?" And Steven went *off*:

"Don't you get it, Mom? That's why I have to leave. I want to find out what it's like to worry about myself for a change. I want to do what I want."

"You get to do what you want. You chose your own college. You chose your major. In another year, you'll be choosing a career. So what in the world are you talking about?"

"Mom, I chose NYU because Annette was going to Juilliard, and she told me we should be in the same city for college. Plus, I wanted to be close to Jeffrey, just in case he . . . just in case. And I thought about going to the Berklee College of Music in Boston anyway, but Dad wanted me to minor in accounting so I'd have *something to fall back on*. Right, Dad?"

"Yes, but —"

"So I kind of chose a college. I kind of chose my major. I guess I'll kind of choose a career. But I'm sick of *kind of* having a life. Plus, no matter where I go, it's not like anybody ever leaves me alone anyway."

"What are you talking about, Steven?" Dad asked. "We've only visited when you've asked us to, and we —"

Steven cut Dad off with a sigh. "It's not you, Dad. And it's not you, either, Mom. It's just . . . look, I want to know what it's like to go through one day of my life without getting three text messages from Annette. How am I supposed to figure out my future if I can't even think on my own for one single day? And then there's Jeffrey."

"Steven . . ." my father said in his scary-dad warning voice.

"No, listen, Dad. I've always done everything for that kid. Right? When he was in the hospital, I always — well, you know all that stuff. But he's been past the five-year point since the beginning of my sophomore year, and I'm still, like, his human crutch. He e-mails me every day, Dad. Every day. 'Steven, what's the answer to this math problem?' 'Steven, do you think the Beatles are cool?' 'Steven, what should I wear to a middle school dance?' And he expects me to answer in real time. You know how many nights I've come home tired after a long day of classes and band practice, and then had to e-mail Jeffrey back before I could start my three hours of studying? So many times I've thought about just blowing him off for a day, just until after the big accounting exam or until I finish the huge paper for English or until I just get some freaking sleep. But then I picture him the way he looked the first time he ever came home from the hospital, when he threw up on my shoes. Remember that?"

It was silent downstairs for a while, and I thought really hard about leaving the closet, closing the door, climbing into bed, and covering my head with my pillow so I'd have no chance of hearing any more. But I stayed.

Dad broke the silence. "Steven, we all remember that. But it was a long time ago, and . . . listen, why don't you just take the semester off and stay around here? Don't roll your eyes, son, I'm serious. I could get you a job at the firm, and you could get an apartment in town. You could earn some money, get a head start on paying back your school loans. We could promise to leave you alone, and Annette . . . well, she would be in New York, wouldn't she? So you could live your life for a while."

"No, I couldn't. Being in town is the worst. Every single person who ever sees me says, 'Hi, Steven. How's your little brother feeling?' Or 'Hi, Steven. How's Annette? Have you popped the question yet?' Nobody ever says, 'Hi, Steven. How are you doing?' I just want to be in a place where people look at me and see me without all this baggage around my neck. Is that so terrible?"

Mom said, "No, it's not so terrible. But . . . Africa? That's so far away."

"That's the point. No computer. No cell phone. Just me and the drums."

Mom's voice broke then. "Steven, I understand why you're upset. We should have understood it a long time ago, I guess. But I don't know whether I can *handle* this. You, out of touch, in *Africa*? You were the child we never had to worry about."

"Well," Steven said, "maybe you should *start* worrying."

My family has always been big on the italics.

The letter assignment was even easier. I banged it out in one sitting a few days later.

TO: drum_master@jerseynet.com
FROM: dangerous_pie@jerseynet.com

Hi Steven —

I know you don't want to hear from me, and that you probably won't even be reading your e-mail until God knows when. But I have some stuff going on, and I just want you to listen. Or at least I want to pretend you're listening.

If you were around, I would have a million questions for you. I feel like this is the most confusing year of my life, and it's only the second week of school. I mean, you know I've always had trouble with the actual *school* part of school, but this year everything else is upside down, too.

I guess the first thing I want to know is, have you ever lied to Mom and Dad? Or not exactly lied, but didn't tell them something really big? I don't want to tell you about it, because you would probably kill me, but I sort of have that kind of situation going on. Anyway, I'm writing to you because Miss Palma is making us write to someone we admire. I picked you, and one thing I have always admired is that you always tell the truth, even when it's hard to do. I can't imagine you would ever keep anything secret from M&D. But then again, I can't picture you breaking up with Annette and running away to Africa, either. I mean, I'm not mad or anything. I'm just wondering if maybe there's other stuff I don't know about you.

Speaking of people who always tell the truth, even when it hurts, Tad is being all weird. He made me make this deal with him: He would tutor me in math and I would train him so he could walk across the stage at eighth-grade graduation. But now he seems all mad at me about it. Plus, there's this new girl in school named Lindsey, and he keeps trying to, like, hook me up with her. I keep telling him that A. I barely know the girl, and B. Why would she go for me? But then he gets all mad at me for that, too. It's almost like he's jealous of me for getting together with her, even though I HAVEN'T EVER GOTTEN TOGETHER WITH HER. Not to mention that if I ever did get together with her, it would be BECAUSE he's pushing me into it.

So we got into an argument in gym, and I'm not sure we're even talking to each other now (I mean, me and Tad. Not me and Lindsey. Or me and you. Because I would be talking to you if I could).

Another thing: Lindsey. This is completely embarrassing, but the worst part is that I do like her. I don't know why, but the second I saw her it was like we were two magnets or something. All I know is I've never felt like this before. Is this what it was like when you met Annette? Did you just know? Did she? What if one person is instantly sure, and the other one is just playing around or something?

And what if the feeling isn't even right? Like with Annette, did you just wake up one day and think she was ugly? Or did she gradually annoy you more and more over time?

Did I?

I'm sorry I bothered you.

> Your little brother,
>
> Jeff

PARTNERS

It's amazing how life works. Sometimes a day feels like three months, but other times weeks fly by without you even really noticing. Tad kept tutoring me, I kept making him use the aerobic equipment, and he kept punishing me for it by forcing me to lift weights. My upper body was sore all the time, and according to Tad his legs were about to fall off any minute from the strain of pedaling an exercise bike for three minutes on the easiest level.

But I was actually doing OK in math, Tad was pedaling every day, and one night I noticed that if I flexed it really hard, I was starting to have something that might one day become a bicep muscle.

Meanwhile, Tad spent half his time trying to get me together with Lindsey and the other half complaining about what a love-struck dork I was. The worst was science, because it was the only class besides gym that we all had together. Sitting at our little table was super-weird. Every time I talked to

Lindsey, Tad just sat there smirking at me. And whenever I wasn't talking to her, I was getting busted by Mr. Laurenzano for not paying attention.

Which wasn't really fair. I was totally paying attention — to the back of Lindsey's elegant, swanlike neck. Anyway, the worst was this one day when we had to pair up for an experiment. Tad made this big show of, *"Don't worry about me, kids. I'll just work by myself in the corner. Or maybe Mr. Laurenzano can pair me up with some other lonely, friendless outcast. You just go ahead and have your fun, though."*

So that's how I became lab partners with Lindsey. Honestly, what would you have done? The experiment was this whole complicated thing where you pushed a toy car down a ramp, timed how long it took to go the distance, tilted the ramp a little more, and repeated until the ramp couldn't tilt any further.

We had only two problems: Lindsey kept making wisecracks, and I was so intoxicated with her presence that I kept forgetting to do stuff. Lindsey was the official car-pusher, and I was the timer. Before the first run, we were supposed to guess what would happen. She said, "Well, I'm going to assume that gravity works pretty much the same on the East Coast as it does in Cali, so I think the car will roll down the ramp. What do you think? And do these lab goggles make my face look fat?"

"Uh, no. Your face is very, um, goggle-worthy. And I think you're probably right about the car."

She beamed at me. "Wow, I'm goggle-worthy. You sure know the way to a girl's heart. Ready, Doctor Alper?"

Then she pushed the car. But I was so distracted that I forgot to push the little button on the timer, so we had to do the whole thing again. Which Lindsey found totally hilarious. "OK," she said. "Are you ready NOW, or do we have to send you back to Button Pushing One-oh-one?"

"Um, what's Button Pushing One-oh-one?"

I was wearing a button-down shirt that day. Lindsey reached out and poked one of the buttons into my chest. "There, *that's* how you push a button. Any questions?"

Yeah, I thought. *Will you marry me?* But of course all I did was stammer and stutter my way through the rest of the period, while my goggles steamed up repeatedly due to nervousness. Meanwhile, across the room, Tad was working with some girl from Guatemala who barely spoke any English. She was probably the perfect partner for him, because from the look on his face, I had a feeling she wouldn't want to know what he was mumbling under his breath every time I looked over there.

All in all, it was an interesting class period. I dropped the timer twice, Mr. Laurenzano told me three times to focus, Lindsey never stopped smiling at me once, and I learned that gravity works the same everywhere. But it wasn't the only form of attraction in that classroom.

On the way out of the room, I said, "Hey, Lindsey? I had fun being your partner."

She punched me on the arm and said, "You ain't seen nothing yet."

Tad said, "Adios, amigos," and rolled off down the hall alone.

During our next workout, I told Tad I thought he was ready to try the treadmill. He refused to even think about it, and climbed right onto the bike. The same thing happened every day for a week or so, until one day when we were about to get on our machines, I finally said, "Tad, you have to practice walking sometime. That's the deal. Otherwise, you're never going to be ready for —"

"Have I ever told you why I stopped walking?"

Whoa, shocker. Tad used to walk at least part of every day until partway through sixth grade. Then all of a sudden, he just gave up and started spending all of his time in a wheelchair. At first, the physical therapist would argue and argue with him about it, but eventually he wore her down. But he had never, ever talked about why he'd quit like that. "No, you never have. But you don't have to if you don't want to —"

"No, you should know this. Remember in sixth grade I had that huge screaming fight with Brianna Slack?"

Oh, I remembered. She was this girl who sometimes sat with us at lunch. Until suddenly, one day
during group work in math, Tad had called her
a "dripping, festering human pus factory" and
"Zitzilla." Then she had run out of math class crying
hysterically. After that, she'd never talked to either
of us again. She still went to our school, but it was
like we were on totally different planets.

"How could I forget? Zitzilla, right?"

He chuckled, but not in a happy way. "Yeah,
Zitzilla. But you probably don't know what she said
to me first."

I waited while Tad looked everywhere but at me.
Then finally he made eye contact and continued.
"Jeff, she asked me why I walked funny. I told her
about the whole cancer thing. She said, *'Yeah, I know
that. And Jeffrey had cancer, too, so he limps — but he
doesn't make that, like, scrunchy face when he walks.
Plus, you stick out your tongue every time you take a
step. How come?'*"

"So what did you say?"

"Dude, you have to understand. Brianna was the first girl I ever thought was, um. Well — never mind. It doesn't matter."

Brianna? I thought. *Tad liked Brianna Slack?* That was odd, because A. He had never mentioned it, and B. She wasn't that cute.

"Ouch," I said.

"Yeah, ouch. So I got a little cranky."

Right. And Mount Saint Helens sometimes gets a little rumbly.

"So you said —"

"I said that if my face looked like someone had been firing yellow crayons into it with a rocket launcher, I wouldn't be making fun of how other people walk. I know I overreacted, but I was so mortified. I mean, I knew I limped, but I had no idea I looked so repulsive while I was doing it."

"So you stopped walking."

"Yup."

"Wow, you really showed her."

Tad flipped me a gesture that wasn't going to earn him any extra points for etiquette. Then he got up out of his chair, and climbed shakily onto the treadmill.

That first time, Tad took nine steps at one mile per hour. It was a start.

Soon enough, it was almost time for the dreaded First Dance of the Year: the Halloween Hop. As if anyone under the age of sixty-five actually knew what a Hop was. Plus, dances are always a horror, but when you combine the usual boy-girl part with the additional menace of picking a costume, you've got a whole new level of angst. Tad and I were discussing it before science class one day. He was pushing hard for matching *Star Wars* outfits: him as R2-D2 and me as C-3PO. Or maybe historical figures, with him as President Franklin D. Roosevelt and me as — whoever. Basically, as long as Tad got to have wheels, he figured we were all set. Personally, I kind of wanted to do my own thing. I had vague visions of dressing up as Lance Armstrong, the perfect costume for a biking cancer survivor. But then there was the whole shiny-shorts thing.

You can see the dilemma.

Of course, in the middle of the whole scene, Lindsey came in and sat down. "Ooh," she said, "you're going to the dance?"

Tad said, "Yup. But my date is being a little difficult."

Lindsey reached across the table and poked Tad's arm. "Who said he's *your* date?" she asked.

Oh, man. The shiny shorts were definitely out. "Uh, so I guess you're going, too?" I said.

"Yuppers. I've got to see how you all get down and party on the East Coast. I've got my outfit picked out and everything."

I didn't get to hear what she'd be wearing, because that's when Mr. Laurenzano came in and started yammering at us. But I wasn't exactly tuned in to his channel. All I could think was *Yikes, I have a date. I think.*

At the end of the period, Tad asked Lindsey a question that would have some serious consequences. "If my boy here is going to be your date, shouldn't you tell him what you'll be wearing so you can coordinate costumes?"

Oh, great, I thought. *We haven't ever been alone together for more than a minute, and already we're going for the matching leisure wear.*

Lindsey said, "You're right, Tad. But I don't want to ruin the mystery completely. So I'll just give you a hint. When you're helping Jeff pick a costume, think Disney."

NIGHT OF THE LIVING WATERFOWL

Miss Palma's next assignment was: Write an episode in your life as though it were being written by a future scholar as part of your biography.

She came as a princess. He came as a duck. The dance should have been a massive disaster, but somehow it worked. Thus, before the great disappointments of his later adolescence, before the terrible ordeals he faced during his second and third years as an eighth grader, Jeffrey Alper had one nearly perfect night.

Legend has it that Lindsey Abraham, despite her famous wit, was secretly a romantic at heart. Perhaps that is why she decided to attend the Halloween festivities at East Village Middle School dressed as Cinderella. Unfortunately, through some miscommunication that has been lost to the sands of time, Jeffrey was only told to dress as a Disney character — without any more specific directions that might have led him to choose a Prince Charming costume. So, after many hours of consultation with his most trusted friend and sometime math tutor, Thaddeus

Ibsen, Jeffrey met Lindsey in the lobby of the school on the night of the dance in a hand-me-down Donald Duck outfit.

Try to imagine, through the mist of the intervening century, the horrifying tableau: She appears from behind a pillar, gorgeous in silk of the palest blue and purest white. He limps in through the double doors, sporting a sailor suit, a jaunty beret, and a bright orange rubber beak. Their eyes meet. He inhales, stunned by the vision before him.

She must be somewhat stunned as well. "Jeffrey?" she asks.

He nods, his duckbill flopping exaggeratedly. There is a moment of total silence. "Well," Jeffrey mumbles defensively, "you *said* I should think Disney."

And then the unexpected occurs. Lindsey Abraham, princess of the ball, throws her head back and laughs. "God, I totally *heart* you. You're just so goofy."

"Donald Duck, actually," Jeffrey says. She laughs some more and holds out her arm. He blushes furiously, but takes it in his own.

Together, they walk through an arch of crepe paper into their first date.

History does not record exactly what is said for most of the next hour, as Jeffrey and Lindsey sit in the gym bleachers,

talking intensely. However, a passing sixth-grade vampire over-
hears the following exchange:

Lindsey: So, do you want to dance?

Jeffrey: Uh, dancing is pretty hard for me because of the . . .
(*gestures vaguely in direction of his bad foot*).

Lindsey: (*Looks concerned, then slowly breaks into a mis-
chievous grin*) So, do you want to slow dance?

That was on a Friday. Tad came over on Saturday,
and grilled me for about an hour before he even
bothered to mention anything about math. On the
one hand, I felt pretty weird discussing Lindsey with
him, especially since he had supposedly come down
with some kind of miraculous last-minute twelve-
hour illness that had kept him away from the dance.
But on the other, I was busting to talk about it with
someone, and Steven was out of the country. As
you might imagine, my parents were an *extremely*
distant third choice.

Tad led off with his usual gentle charm. "So, D.A.,
how was the dance? Was Lindsey all over you like a

shag carpet? Was she totally hot for your duck-billed bod? Did you sneak her into the workout room like I told you to? Did you, like, make out on my favorite exercise bike? 'Cause I'd really want to be warned before Monday if you guys, like, drooled all over my seat. I mean, there *are* those disinfecting wipes hanging on the wall by the free weights, but —"

"Dude, it wasn't like that."

"Oh, you wiped the seat?"

"NO! I mean, you might find this hard to believe, but we mostly talked."

"Excellent! You were suavely laying the ground-work for seduction. That's good technique right there. Did you whisper in her ear? Chicks love that. At least from what I've read in certain illicit —"

"Tad, it wasn't like *that*, either. We had *the talk*."

He pretended to be wiping tears from the corners of his eyes. "Oh, wow, she told you how babies are made? I kind of thought the stork thing might satisfy you for a few more years, but I suppose my little Jeffy boy is growing up. If you have any follow-up questions, I'd be happy to refer you to a few choice Web sites."

"Not *that* talk. I told her about . . . you know."

"The Pythagorean theorem? The FOIL method? Photosynthesis?"

"Would you stop being such a snapperhead for a minute? I told her about my cancer, all right?"

Tad shut up for a little while. Then in a much mellower voice, he asked, "So how did *that* go over?"

"I don't know. I think it went OK. She danced with me afterward . . . and . . ."

"And what?" Tad asked as a smirk started spreading across his face. It's amazing how hard it is for him to be serious for more than three seconds.

"And then I *did* take your advice about the weight room."

Tad's smirk reached epic proportions, and his eyebrows shot up so high it looked like he had just been given a face-lift with a construction crane.

"Oh, shut up," I said. "It was totally N.B.D." Tad and I say "N.B.D." all the time; it means "No Big Deal."

Amazingly, Tad settled down again. "What exactly did you tell her?"

"Um, well, she knew about it already. Apparently, after the first day of school, she asked a couple of girls about me."

"Holy — she was asking around about you. That's, like, major." He held out his fist for me to pound. I pounded it, and continued.

"And it turns out her grandmother is a breast cancer survivor. So she knew the basics, and she was so cool about everything. I mean, I couldn't even believe we were having this conversation, you know? It's funny how you can worry about something for so long, and then when it finally happens, it's almost no biggie.

"Oh, there was one thing. She wanted to know whether I had been in remission for five years yet, and I told her yes."

Tad looked bummed out when I said that, because he wasn't past his five-year anniversary. "I'm sorry, man," I said. "But she asked, so —"

"Whatever, dude. What else did she want to know?"

"She asked about my limp, so I explained about drop foot. But I also told her about my bike riding, so she wouldn't think I was, uh . . ."

"Crippled?"

Ouch. "Well, yeah."

"Did you tell her about your school stuff?"

"Kind of. She asked what the deal was with you and me in gym, so then I thought I should explain our pact. Is that OK?"

"Oh, sure, since you were speaking of cripples anyway."

What do you say to that? "Tad, what's your problem? If I'm going to be, like, sharing things with Lindsey, how could I not tell her about something as major as that?"

"Oooohhh, you're *sharing things* with Lindsey. Should I bust out my guitar so we can all sing 'Kumbaya'? Sharing things. Geez."

"I don't see what the problem is. I was just being honest."

"Well, it's easy to be honest about *your* late effects, D.A. You know, 'Lindsey, I have a cute little limp. But I'm fine. And sometimes I space out in class. But it's all good. My friend Tad, on the other hand? He's a mess. Can you believe he needs a testosterone shot every day? Plus, human growth hormone so he won't be totally deformed when he grows up — IF he grows up?'"

"Tad, I didn't tell her all that! All I told her was that you were tutoring me so I could pass the math test, and that you were going to walk across the stage at graduation."

"Dude, what if I don't walk across the stage? Why would I want anyone to know about that? Did it ever occur to you that I might not want the whole world to watch me prove I'm just as crippled as ever?"

"Look, I told Lindsey how I can't do math to save my life. I don't see how it's different. If you're going to be honest, you have to be totally honest."

"So of course you told her how you threw out the letter, right?"

I didn't say anything.

"So you didn't tell her about the letter? That wasn't very *honest* of you."

For the millionth time, I forced myself to take a deep breath. Then I said, "Hey, uh, can we just work on math for a while?"

"Absolutely." He booted up his laptop and put it on the table in front of us. "But while we're waiting . . . *is* there anything I should know about the seat on the exercise bike?"

I smiled. "Maybe," I said. "Maybe."

Tad punched me, and we got to work.

THE END OF THANKSGIVING

Over the next few weeks, Lindsey and I spent every spare moment talking. Or texting. Or IM'ing. Basically, we did everything but connect our houses with two cans and a string. I found out so much amazing stuff about her that I don't even know where to begin. I guess a list makes as much sense as anything else, so here goes.

AMAZING STUFF ABOUT LINDSEY

- Moved from California because of her dad's job. He's a digital effects designer, and Lindsey knows how to make movies on a computer. Her name was even in the credits of a movie once.

- Her supposed BFF from California started out e-mailing her every day, but now they're running out of things to talk about, and the messages have slowed down to maybe one or two a week. (Who could run out of things to talk about with Lindsey? I told L. that her "friend" must be an idiot.)

- Misses Cali oranges the most; insists that Florida ones aren't as sweet. Promised to let me do a taste test someday.

- Loves baseball, is a huge Angels fan. When I told her I love the Yankees, she went into a whole speech about their lame payroll-to-wins ratio. Really knows the sport. Favorite color: red. Looks hot in Angels jersey, but I will never admit it.

- Has one older brother named David, who's away at college. Actually *likes* having both parents to herself.

- Says I'm different from other guys because when I met her, I didn't check out her body. Or as she put it, "You actually looked at my face. I *love* that." I changed the subject before my truth-telling compulsion could burst her bubble.

- Knows how to surf and ski. Has never shoveled snow.

- Thinks Tad is "sweet, deep down inside." I was like, "Dude, I think you'd have to be doing some *serious* exploratory drilling before you found Tad's sweet spot." But I am glad she likes him OK.

Speaking of Tad, he was doing a great job of helping me with my math, plus I was up to three sets of curls with ten-pound weights by Thanksgiving. AND I got an eighty-six on my first report card in math. I know that probably doesn't sound so high to you, but for me it was a total world record. My father practically wet himself.

In other news, Tad walked across the entire exercise room the day before Thanksgiving. He could barely breathe when he sat down on the weight bench afterward, but he was smiling from ear to ear as he gasped, "Twenty-two steps!" Again, not such a Guinness moment for most people, but in Tad-steps, that's like a mile and a half.

So everything was going great, which is why I should have known we were in trouble. But I let my guard down, and BOOM!

Before I tell you what happened, I have to tell you something about me. A couple of years ago, we got a phone call. In the middle of mowing his lawn, our Grampa Pete had slumped over the mower and died of a heart attack. Steven went into hysterics. I mean *serious* hysterics — like, he couldn't even breathe. I think I probably cried some — I really loved Grampa Pete — but I didn't lose my mind like Steven did.

When Steven got calmed down, he looked at me and said, "What? Aren't you even upset?"

I was like, "Of course I'm upset. I'm just not *surprised*." That's yet another thing about cancer. See, most kids who haven't had it think that their normal, everyday lives are safe, that their parents' jobs are secure, their grandparents won't die without a warning, the stock market won't crash. Their mom and dad won't get divorced. Their family pets won't run out in the street and go SPLAT. Most kids, even though they don't realize it, believe they live in a plastic bubble.

But most of my earliest memories are of spinal taps, throwing up for two hours straight on my birthday, watching my own hair fall out while my friends were worried about learning how to write their names in crayon. And I guess Steven has had a lot of those shocks, too, through being my brother. But that's still not the same as being me. I remember this other time, Steven came down to the hospital in Philadelphia with me, and found out that another leukemia patient had died. Her name was Samantha, and I don't remember much about her, except that she used to play Go Fish with me. Anyway, Steven went absolutely ballistic. I think they might have even had to give him tranquilizers. I was sad and all, but even at the age of five, I was also a little bit like, *Duh! What do you think happens on the cancer ward when you're not here? It ain't all snow cones and Ping-Pong tournaments.*

Wow, it never occurred to me until just now that maybe I'm a bit more grown-up than my brother is. He still thinks life is supposed to make sense. I mean, I know it's not easy to be like Tad, who constantly thinks the whole planet is zooming toward some kind of gigantic cosmic toilet. But skipping around being all jolly is just asking the world to smack you upside the head with a tennis racket.

Which is what happened to me the day after Thanksgiving break.

Can you believe it all started with a candy heart?

Thanksgiving Day was pretty odd, because it was the first year Steven hadn't been around. Come to think of it, it was the first time Annette hadn't been over for at least part of the time. Mom made her usual huge turkey-with-every-single-side-dish-in-the-universe meal, and Dad and I ate as much as we possibly could. But without Steven's bottomless-pit stomach around, we barely made a dent in the mounds of food.

There's no sadder sight than Mom's homemade pumpkin pie with only three pieces missing.

Steven called after dinner, but the connection was really bad. He had stayed up until three AM so he could call us during dessert, which was sort of nice, at least. It was only the third or fourth time I had talked to him since September, so there was a ton I wished I could say. But with my parents standing there, and my memory of that horrible convo he had had with them floating around in my head, I didn't say much of anything. Most of the call was just him blabbing on and on about all the amazing drum skills he was learning, and how cool all the drummers from around the world were.

Oh, and apparently he saw some zebras.

I couldn't imagine ditching Lindsey and my family for a bunch of stripey horses and some bongos, but whatever.

The day after that, Mom went shopping and Dad worked. I rode my bike over to Tad's and we hung out for a while playing violent video games. I'm more of a race car–game guy, but Tad loves to blow things up. Shocker, right? Then Tad's mom made leftover turkey sandwiches for me, Tad, and the E.R.C. That's what Tad calls his eight-year-old sister, Yvonne. It stands for "Emergency Replacement Child." She was born less than a year after Tad was first diagnosed, so he insists his parents only had her in case he didn't survive.

After lunch, just so he would give me credit for trying hard, I asked Tad if he thought maybe we should do some math. He said I deserved the weekend off. So I told him in that case maybe I'd ride on over to Lindsey's. Then he got all mad and said he wasn't just some kind of twenty-four-hour on-call math service. I told him I knew that, and pointed out that I had just spent the morning machine-gunning random pretend mercenaries with him, but when I left he was still sulking.

When I got to Lindsey's, nobody was even home. I stood on her porch like an idiot, ringing her bell every minute or so, until I remembered she and her dad were going for the weekend to visit her brother at college. I know, I know. How could I forget something that big?

Can you say "methotrexate"?

So I rode my bike for miles and miles, then spent the rest of the day bored out of my skull at home. I repeated the whole ugly cycle for the next two days — the only difference was that the turkey in the sandwiches kept getting older and drier. If there hadn't been any school on Monday, I think I would have been eating green turkey jerky, and died of food poisoning.

But no, there was the whole candy heart thing to contend with instead. When I got to homeroom, my teacher told me to report to the guidance office and see Dr. Galley. She's new this year, or at least sort of new. She was around when my brother was in middle school, but then took the last couple of years off to get an advanced degree. I knew all this because, believe it or not, Steven stayed in touch with her by e-mail. Which is more than he did with me.

I hadn't seen her since the first year of my treatment. All I remembered was that she had soft, blond hair that didn't quite match her tough-sounding voice. Plus, I knew Steven had an old in-joke with her: He always said that if she offered him a candy heart, he would run away in terror. Apparently she only busted out with the candy hearts right when she was about to tell you some horrible news. I knew Steven thought she was awesome, but truthfully, as I walked into her office I was kind of scared.

I sat down in the hard plastic chair next to her desk, and she swiveled to face me. The blond hair had gone partly white, but other than that, she looked very much the same. She smiled at me and said, "Would you like a candy heart?"

Yikes.

"Uh, no, thank you."

She smiled warmly, like a happy grandmother. "So. Jeffrey Alper. I can't believe how grown-up you are. I'm Dr. Galley. I don't know whether you remember me, but I could never forget you. I can't believe you're that same little boy with the baseball cap from your brother's All-City jazz band concert." At this point, her eyes got all misty, and I almost got myself ready to hand her a tissue, but then she recovered. "I've kept meaning to call you down just to say hello, but with four hundred students on my caseload and all this testing to deal with . . ." She swept her hand in a circle to indicate the huge piles of official-looking boxes all around the little room. What perfect decor for a counselor's office — nothing says *Relax* like a million standardized test booklets.

"Anyway, I'm really happy to see you again, looking so big, strong, and healthy. How is your eighth-grade year going so far?"

She sat there perfectly still, smiling and waiting for my answer. It was unnerving. If genetic scientists ever cross an elderly homemaker and a praying mantis, the result will look a whole lot like Dr. Galley. Oh, boy. This woman knew something. But what?

"Oh, fine, fine. Thanks for asking." I looked down into my lap and folded my hands.

"That's great to hear. I've been looking over your five-oh-four plan, and I see that you have faced some academic challenges in the past. But your first marking period grades look good. I haven't heard any complaints from your teachers, either."

She stared. I twiddled my thumbs. She stared some more. When I couldn't take it anymore, I grabbed my backpack, started to stand up, and said, "OK, then, since everything's going so well, I guess I'll just head on back upstairs. It was really great seeing you again, but I have science first period, and I wouldn't want to miss any —"

"Jeffrey, I just got off the phone with your mother."

Wham! My butt hit that chair again so hard my teeth rattled. I suddenly remembered this time in sixth grade when Jimmy Blasingame got called downstairs, and the counselor told him his father had been in a car accident. "Is everything all right? Is Steven OK? What happened?"

It was weird — even though I've been mad at my brother for months, he was the very first person I worried about. I guess even if your idol drops you like a radioactive hot potato, that doesn't mean you want them to get squashed by a charging rhino. Or mauled by a lion. Or even bitten by the deadly green mamba snake. Unless those are in South America, not Africa.

I shook my head to clear it, and Dr. Galley said, "Everybody in your family is fine. I was just calling up the parents of all my students with five-oh-four plans to discuss the upcoming testing, and I surprised your mother a bit. Do you want to guess what she and I figured out?"

Surprised my mother a bit? What did she — oh, geez. "Uh, the square root of negative one?"

"Try again, Jeff."

I felt the breath leave me in a *whoosh*. I swallowed, then said, "Does it have to do with the new promotion requirement?"

"Bingo!" she said, and pushed the candy hearts across the desk again. This time, I took one.

GROUNDED, SORTA

That Dr. Galley is wasting her talents as a school counselor. Really, she should be an interrogator for the army. I tried to resist, but at the first sign of pressure, I spilled like a waterlogged piñata. Then she called my mom. By the time I got home from school, I was almost surprised there wasn't a WANTED: JEFFREY ALPER poster plastered across the front door.

As it turned out, that was only because my parents weren't home yet. Mom got there first, right when I was in the middle of making oatmeal. She started in on me right away, and wouldn't even give me a one-minute cease-fire to finish the crucial sweetening procedure. As a result, I rushed the tasting part, and ended up burning the roof of my mouth to shreds. "Jeffrey Alper," she screeched, "how *could* you? Did you think you'd be able to hide this from us forever, just by getting rid of the letter? Did you ever think about what would happen when you failed the state test?"

Ooh, that made me mad. Unfortunately, my singed palate took away some of the power of my argument. "Gak's not gair! Goo gon't know I'n gonna kail ga kest! Why gon't goo hag any kaith in me?"

The weird thing is, Mom understood what I said anyway. "It *is* fair, Jeff. I *do* have faith in you — usually. But how am I supposed to react when you deliberately deceive your parents? Plus, I'm sorry to say this, but there is a chance you might fail that test."

I swished some water around my mouth until I could talk again. Then I replied, "But I fixed the whole situation. Tad has been doing a great job tutoring me. Come on — you know I got an eighty-six in math this marking period. I'll be fine."

"Maybe, Jeffrey. But I've been teaching for a long time, and I've seen plenty of kids pass my class and still fail the state test. Those tests don't always match up with what kids learn in their courses."

"So what do you want me to do about it? If the test doesn't measure what I'm learning in school, what's the point?"

She sighed. "Jeff, don't get me started on the testing

system. This is not the time to make me even more irritated; plus, it's irrelevant. You have to pass that test, and we have to come up with a real plan for making that happen. Do you understand me?"

I played with my oatmeal. Mom hates that.

"I said, do you understand me?"

I played some more. Did you know that if you stir hot cereal really fast in a circle, you can make a little steam tornado?

Mom grabbed my wrist. "Jeffrey —"

"Do we have to tell Dad?"

"What do you mean? Of course we have to tell Dad. Why on earth wouldn't I —"

"Mom, he's the whole reason I stuffed that stupid letter down the disposal in the first place."

"You stuffed it down the disposal? It was recyclable!"

"Uh, Mom, can you please focus? I stuffed the letter down the disposal because Dad already hates me enough without *this* hanging over everything."

"What are you talking about?"

"Mom, you're kidding, right? Haven't you ever noticed how mad your husband gets whenever your son has trouble with math? I knew if he saw the letter, he'd, like, chain me to a desk and make me do worksheets twelve hours a night. AND he'd run out and get me some super-expensive tutor. Then he'd spend the whole year making critical comments about how *Jeffrey's condition will send us to the poorhouse yet!* whenever you guys think I can't hear. Plus, he'd still insist on 'helping' me with the math himself. And he'd explode at me every fifteen seconds about how lazy and unmotivated I am."

"Do you really think your father would do all that?"

"Have you *met* my father, Mom?"

"Oh, Jeffrey. I know it's hard for you to understand, but your father loves you more than you will ever know. He just sometimes has a hard time showing it. And he gets so *frustrated* when you have so much trouble. But he's not frustrated at *you*."

I snorted.

"Jeff, do you remember the first meeting we had with your fourth-grade teacher, when she told us you were falling behind in math?"

"Uh, I believe the actual phrase was *hopelessly* behind."

"Yeah, well . . . after you went to bed that night, and after Steven was safely locked away in his room, do you know what your father did?"

"Um, try to sell me on eBay?"

"No, he did *not* try to sell you on eBay! He cried, Jeffrey. He cried."

"*Dad* cried? About me?"

"Oh, buddy. Your father adores you. He just worries about you so much. You have to understand: No parent ever wants to see his child struggle. And it's even harder for Dad to see you struggle with math, because that's always come so easy to him." She sighed again. "Jeff, do you know how Steven always gets really impatient with us when he tries to explain some drumming concept and we don't get it right away? That's how your dad is about math. It's so natural for him that he just can't see why it wouldn't be that easy for everyone. And he wants it to be easy for *you* — not because he thinks you're stupid, or lazy, or anything else. Just because he wants his son to succeed. For your father, numbers have always been the path to success. He wants you to have that, too."

"So you don't think he's going to, like, ground me until I'm thirty?"

"Nope," Mom said. "*I* am."

The next day at lunch, I tried to fill Tad in on the whole fiasco. "Your mom grounded you until the test?"

I nodded.

"And then she said WHAT?" he practically shouted.

"Shhh," I whispered. "It's embarrassing!"

"But she really called you retar —"

"Yes, Tad, my mother called me 'retarded.' Are you happy now?"

"In those exact words?"

"Pretty much."

"Tell me the whole thing from the beginning."

"Well, I already told you everything that happened when I got home. And then my father came in the front door, so I went up to my room. I listened from my closet, and they had this big argument."

"And your mom was just all, like, *'Honey, the boy's a retard'*?"

"Kind of. My mom told him about the test, and the letter, and he said, 'Jeffrey *will* pass that exam.' So she said, 'I don't know. Something like a quarter of my students failed their math statewides last year.' Then my dad goes, 'I'm telling you, Jeffrey isn't a quarter of your students. He's Jeffrey Alper, and he is NOT going to get held back in eighth grade.'"

"So she thought you *might* fail. That's not the same as —"

"Would you let me finish? Then my mom goes, 'No matter how hard you try, you can't just wish Jeffrey into passing this thing.' So my dad said something I didn't quite hear, and then my mom kind of shouted, 'No, YOU listen! I'm going right up to that school tomorrow, and I'm going to tell them to appeal this all the way to the state. In his three years there, Jeffrey has never failed ANYTHING. So how can they hold him back on the basis of one day of testing? It's not right.' So my father goes, 'You can't do that. Jeffrey has to stand on his own two feet in this world. If he can't pass the test, then maybe he doesn't belong in high school.' I could hear my mom pacing the floor, smacking her hands together, and then she said, 'Honey, I know you've never believed in Jeffrey's disability —' and he said, 'That's not the point. Disability or not, he still needs to —' and she said, 'It IS the point! They can't use this test to ruin my child's future. For God's sake, he has brain damage! The counselor said the only students who would be exempt from this new rule are the developmentally disabled kids, but I don't see what the difference is. How can they hold a child responsible for having a brain injury?'"

"Whoa, Jeff. Then what happened?"

"I don't know. The phone rang, and it was Steven. So my parents pretended nothing was wrong, and by the time they got done talking with him it was dinnertime. I didn't say anything to either of them the whole meal, and neither of them was talking too much, either. Then, as soon as I could, I went for a long bike ride."

"Dude, it was, like, twelve degrees out last night."

"Well, I'd rather freeze to death than sit in my house and listen to my parents talking about how stupid I am. Plus, it was thirty-eight. And I wore a hat. And anyway, my grounding starts today, so I figured it was my last chance to ride for a while."

"Big difference. Anyway, your mom didn't say you were a retarded kid. She just said your situation wasn't that different from theirs."

"OK, that's fine, then. Tad, you're not the ugliest kid in the world. You just look like him."

"Ha-ha. Don't be bitter, Jeff. That's my job."

Just then, Lindsey came over and sat down next to me. "Hi, Tad!" she said. "Hi, Jeff! Hey, I'm not interrupting anything, am I?"

"Uh, no," I said. "We were just ... I mean, Tad was ... uh, nope."

"So what were you guys talking about?"

"Well," I said, "it's very complicated. We were discussing . . . umm . . . hats. You know, hats. Like, the head kind."

"There's another kind?" Lindsey asked.

"Hey, Jeff?" Tad said. "If your mom needs any evidence to prove that you're retarded, let me know. I'd be glad to record you talking to Lindsey. I'm pretty sure that would do the trick."

In English that day, we started a new unit on drama and "the world of the theatre." I know that in America, it's spelled "theater," but somehow you could just hear the "-re" at the end of the word when Miss Palma said it. Miss Palma got so excited telling us about the first play we were going to read that I thought she might pass out right in the middle of our warm-up activity. She said it was her favorite literary work of all time. Then she put the back of her hand against her brow and said, "Oh, I'm sorry, Mister Shakespeare!" She went on to tell us that this play, *Cyrano de Bergerac*, was about a French knight dude with a huge nose who falls in love with an impossible-to-get beautiful girl named Roxanne. Of course, Roxanne's in love with a really good-looking dumb guy named Christian, because let's face it, why would she be into the guy with the schnoz? Well, when he's not busy being a hero, Cyrano is also a famous poet. So he makes a deal that he will pretend to be Christian and write a bunch of love letters to Roxanne.

I know you'll be shocked to hear that it all ends badly.

Anyway, all the other guys in the class were complaining that we had to read a love story, but a lot of them calmed down when Miss Palma told them the play had a sword duel and a war in it, with cannons and everything. Plus, she promised that at least one character would die a painful, violent death, which sounded promising.

At our tutoring session that night (of course, my parents said I could still slave away over math even while I was grounded from everything else in the world), Tad was all worked up about *Cyrano*. "Jeff," he said, "did you hear what she said about how the ugly guy gets the girl by pretending to be the stud-master? I can totally do that. I'll just get a girlfriend online!"

"And what good would that do you, exactly?"

"I don't know, maybe she'd fall so madly in love with my personality that she wouldn't get all freaked out later on when we met in person and I was all gimped out."

"Uh, Tad, I don't mean to be all, like, ego-deflating, but A. I'm not sure your personality is a massive tourist attraction, and B. It's not like you're having some genius news flash. *Everybody* lies online. It's expected. In fact, if I were a girl in some chat room and you told me you were some kind of chick-magnet, I'd automatically think the opposite of what you said. Like, you'd go, 'I'm a six-foot-tall football player with stormy blue eyes,' and she'd go, 'Aha, a mousy-brown midget.' Or you'd tell her, 'In my spare time, I enjoy helping out poor South American orphans by building them sturdy wooden tree-dwellings,' and she'd think, 'Swell, yet another computer geek who's never left his room, much less the continental United States.'

"And eventually, you'd have to meet in person. So you'd be all nervous about the wheelchair, until she walked in and you found out she was actually a Siamese twin with only half a head or something."

"You're probably right," Tad said. "And she'd go, 'Tad? I've had my eye on you for a long time, but now I've got half a mind to just leave you here.'"

I groaned. "Dude, that's terrible!"

"Well anyway, I still think I could learn a lot from this Cyrano guy. Like, what about the whole beau geste thing?"

"Uh, what are you talking about? What's a 'bow zhest'?"

"Didn't you pay attention during the unit vocab definitions? A beau geste is a beautiful gesture — like throwing your coat down over a puddle so a fair damsel can walk on it and keep her feet dry."

"OK, so this is important why?"

"Well, haven't you ever wished that, just once, you could do something completely magnificent?"

"Dude, mostly I just hope I won't forget to zip my pants in the morning. Or trip and fall down the front steps of the school."

"Oh, come on, Jeff. Don't you ever want to do something grand to impress — I don't know — Lindsey?"

"I guess. Maybe. I don't know. It's kind of hard to do anything really impressive when you're chubby, brain-damaged, and grounded forever. Why?"

"I'm just saying, I think it would be awesome to do something larger than life, something people would talk about for a long time." Tad was staring out the window of my family room into space, and I shuddered to think of what insane stunts he could come up with if I didn't get him off the subject.

"Whatever, Tad. You know what would be a really *beau* thing for us to do right now? We could study mathematics, the beautiful and fascinating science of numbers."

So we got to work. But I should have realized that once Tad gets an idea in his head, he's on it like a pit bull with a bad case of lockjaw.

CHALLENGES

Between then and Christmas vacation, school was crazy. Tad was staying on the exercise bike a little longer each day, and I was pumping iron and doing word problems. Meanwhile, the classwork was piling on. Every teacher made some huge project due the last week, even though half the kids were missing tons of class time because of holiday concert practice. We also took a gigantic pretest for the statewides, which came as a surprise. The teachers all said not to worry too much, that they had purposely given us no advance warning because they wanted to see what we really knew without a whole flurry of test preparation.

Yeah, I never find it stressful when I suddenly have to drop everything and spend twelve hours taking a surprise exam.

As soon as I saw the actual cartons of booklets being wheeled into my homeroom, I realized, *Oh, those are the boxes from Dr. Galley's office*. And then I thought, *Hey! She totally knew this was coming, and THAT is why she checked in with my parents. But none of them told me.*

So you can imagine my mood by the time I was finishing the math portion, which took most of the second day. Then we had some nutty rearranged schedule that sent me to English class. Because I get extra time on tests to help make up for my "educational challenges," I walked in late. An extremely popular preppy girl was just reading the class the last sentence of her journal entry.

The assignment on the board was: Cyrano de Bergerac faces tremendous challenges and pressures but refuses to compromise. Write about a time when you had to face a challenge head-on.

Apparently, the popular girl's answer to this question hadn't sat well with Tad. A few minutes later, Miss Palma called on him, and he started reading:

"Hi, everybody. Thank you for listening to my journal about challenges. I have faced some terrible ones, but I have always, like, totally come through. I am really exceptionally awesome.

"Like this one time, my friend Muffy was planning a big sleepover party on a Friday night, but she wasn't going to invite my other friend, Madison. Naturally, this put me in a bad place. I thought and thought about what to do. I mean, Muffy throws really amazing parties, so I didn't want to miss it. But on the other hand, I knew that if Madison found out I had gone, I would be so dead the next time I saw her. So what I did was, I pretended I had leprosy for the weekend, but then it got better. On the Friday night, my mom and I went shopping in this mall an hour away instead!

"On Monday, everybody felt so sorry for me being a temporary leper and all. Plus, I got this amazing Kate Spade purse.

"And another time, I was supposed to have swimming in gym, but it was the day of a dance, and I had gotten my hair all done already. I was all, *What am I going to do? Chlorine is, like, the kryptonite of hair. But being unprepared for gym is, like, the kryptonite of my grade point average.* There was only one thing to do:

I went up to Mr. McGrath and told him I couldn't go in the water because I was having my —"

"That's ENOUGH, Mr. Ibsen!" Miss Palma roared. Wow, I hadn't even known she could roar. From the look on Tad's face, neither had he. "Look, Tad, I know you've faced some, um, unusually challenging situations, but that doesn't give you the right to mock other people's journal entries. Just because you have suffered doesn't mean that your fellow students haven't. This room is supposed to be a safe place for sharing thoughts and feelings. But then you go and make a mockery of other students' pain. Why?"

Tad didn't say anything. Which was kind of a first.

Miss Palma continued. "Never mind. Tad, from this point on, you are not allowed to share anything you've written until you show it to me first. And I will allow you to read your words out loud only if they add to the class discussion, if they don't make fun of anybody else, AND if they are an honest reflection of your thoughts and feelings."

Tad nodded. "Fine," he muttered. Then even more quietly, he mouthed, "*Be that way.*"

"Oh, and one more thing: Please redo this entry and have it on my desk tomorrow morning, first thing." She turned her back on Tad, and tried to smile at the rest of the group. But you could still see that her teeth were all clenched up. "All right, now. Does anybody else feel like sharing?"

The whole rest of the class just sat there like they were auditioning for roles in *Night of the Eighth-Grade Zombies*. Finally, Miss Palma announced that we would have the rest of the period for silent reading and reflection, which she always called "R&R."

I opened the file on my computer that has all my social studies notes, and tried to study. Tad kept IM'ing me, though. After a day of high-pressure math, and his ugly scene with my favorite teacher, I really wasn't in the mood. But then an e-mail message popped up and I realized he was sending me his new answer to the journal question:

SO, you want to hear about a challenge? Maybe I should write about the challenge of being a seven-year-old with a brain tumor, although if you don't mind having your head sawed open, that's not really so bad. I will admit that the challenge of being a nine-year-old with a recurrent brain tumor is harder, because then the sawing isn't enough. On the other hand, if you don't mind projectile vomiting for weeks on end or glowing in the dark a little, then maybe you won't think chemotherapy or radiation is so tough, either.

Ooh, I know one. How about coming home from the hospital with a giant hole in your skull, and finding that your own parents have replaced you with a cute little healthy baby while you were under the knife? Because, you know, they didn't *think* they would lose you, but better safe than sorry.

Not that any of those things can compare with coming back to school for sixth grade, after years of being absent all the time, and finding out that everybody is scared to be friends with you.

That's right, scared. Maybe they're afraid that what

you have is contagious, and if they share their pretzels with you on the bus, a gigantic glistening lump o' death will start growing into the side of their brain. Or maybe they're worried that other kids will think they're freaks if they're seen hanging out with a kid who can't even walk right.

Or maybe my mom is right, and their biggest fear is that they will get close to you again, and you'll go and drop dead. So they'll have to totally rearrange their lunchroom seating plans again.

Which is *such* a hassle.

Geez. I had a weird feeling that this wasn't exactly the tone Miss P. was expecting. On the other hand, he was completely right. When you're actually in treatment, you're like the town mascot. Everybody is rooting for you, and helping out with a million fund-raisers for your treatment, and sending you class sets of get-well cards with cute little crayon illustrations for your hospital-room wall. But kids don't have the greatest attention spans. I mean, come on — *people* don't have the greatest attention spans. So they can only sit around worrying about you for so long. Then, gradually, your illness becomes old news, until all you are is an empty seat.

Thinking about it made me feel sorry for Tad, almost. On the other hand, nobody owes you their friendship, either. Even though I knew it wouldn't help my headache, I IM'ed Tad:

Dangerous_pie:	Yeah, you're right. But you can earn your way back into the circle.
Tadditude:	Thanks, Yoda. Then a Jedi will I be?
Dangerous_pie:	Oh, stop. You were trying to come up with a grand gesture, right? I've got a grand gesture for you: Be nice.
Tadditude:	I'm nice to you.
Dangerous_pie:	Meh.
Tadditude:	I can be nice, you snapperhead. Watch me. I'll be so sweet your teeth will hurt.

That's when the real challenge began. On the way out of the room, Tad apologized to Miss Palma, then turned to shoot me a blazing glare. In the hallway, he held the door for a sixth grader. Going down the wheelchair ramp in front of the building, he got hit in the stomach with a Frisbee. He winced, but instead of getting all hissy like he normally would, he flicked the disk to the nearest player. With a smile.

"Nice one," I said.

"Bite me," Tad replied.

That night was supposed to be my last tutoring session before the holiday. When Tad arrived at my house, I almost died of shock. There was a steaming platter of chocolate chip cookies in his lap, and he was struggling to hold on to a container of eggnog while using both hands to roll himself along. My mom grabbed the cookies, and Tad smiled up at her like a Christmas angel.

"You know, Mrs. Alper, I suddenly realized today that I've never really thanked you for all the kindness you've shown me. And I also want to thank you for raising my best friend."

Make me puke, I thought. Mom looked rather startled, but she's pretty smooth socially, so she said, "Why, thank you, Thaddeus. Come on into the house and we'll get down some mugs for this." She shouted for my dad to come downstairs, and he got the exact same treatment from Tad. But knowing how phony the whole charade was, I didn't even want to take the stupid eggnog.

Except I really like eggnog. Tad knows it, too, the rat.

When we finally got around to work, I raised an eyebrow in his direction. "What?" he said. "Can't a guy be appreciative?"

I snorted.

"No, I'm serious. You inspired me today with your totally rude and unsympathetic remarks. From now on, I am going to be kind to everybody — *that's* my beau geste. And if the people around me keep acting like total snapperheads anyway, I am going to harden my heart and be bitter until the day I die. Now, turn your workbook to page twelve. *Please.*"

JOY TO THE WORLD

Hi Steven —

I hope you're staying warm over there. Or cool, if it's hot in the Africa hemisphere. Whatever. I just mean it's weird to celebrate Christmas without you. Tonight Uncle Neil did all his famous impressions, but they didn't feel as funny without you doing the little *ba-dump-bump* drum thing on the table after the punch lines.

I scored big with the presents, but you know I've never really been into presents. Remember that first Christmas after my diagnosis, when everybody gave me mounds of toys and video games for the hospital? But my favorite part was playing snowball fights with our cousins and then you carrying me to bed.

No snow this year.

I have a ton to tell you again, if you ever stop banging on hollow logs long enough to read your mail — not that

I'll ever send this anyway. Things are crazy here. I have a girlfriend. A girlfriend! Remember that girl Lindsey that Mom was teasing me about during that one phone call, but then you had to go because of the monsoon or whatever you call it? Well, she likes me. And I like her. Can you believe we gave each other presents today? Mom and Dad made her come here because of the whole grounding issue (long story), but at least they let us take a walk to the park so we could get a break from Mom chasing us around with hot cocoa and a video camera. Speaking of cameras, Lindsey had been taking pictures of me all week at school, but wouldn't tell me why.

So we exchanged gifts. I got her a box of oranges in a cool crate that says IMPORTED FROM CALIFORNIA on the side. Long story, but she made me share one with her right there in the empty gazebo. It's pretty messy eating an orange with ski gloves on, but we had fun. I had given her my usual speech about how presents don't mean much, and she shouldn't go to any trouble, blah, blah, blah. She didn't listen. First, she whipped out a rectangular gift about the size of a lunch box. There were little reindeer riding bikes on the wrapping paper, which I thought was cool.

I felt like Lindsey really understood me, you know?

But then I opened the box, and there it was: a Hello Kitty bicycle horn, bright pink. It was ghastly. Lindsey said, "Do you like it? I saw it and thought of you because of the whole bike . . . you know . . . uh, Jeff? Say something?"

So she gave me these puppy-dog eyes, and I forced myself to smile and say, "Uh, it's perfect! Thanks, Linds. I'll get this onto my bike, um, right away!"

Then she busted out laughing. "I'm kidding, silly! It's just a joke. I would never make you put that on your bike. But here's for being a good sport!" And she fed me a chunk of orange. Juice got all over my face, but then Lindsey wiped it off with her mitten. I know it sounds strange, but it was definitely — I don't know — a moment.

She had a real present for me: a whole album of photos of me and her, somehow digitally edited together with funny things. One had her face on Cinderella, and mine on Donald Duck. Another had her as the Little Mermaid, and me as Goofy. She really went with the whole Disney theme (another long story).

But the last photo was just me with a heart around it. I was kind of mortified. I mean, if Tad ever sees this thing, I'll be hearing about it until forever. Still, the whole thing is strangely cool: Lindsey sees me as a guy in a heart.

We finally had to go back to the house before A. Mom sent out a search-and-rescue team, or B. The orange juice all over our faces and gloves froze us to death. Then something happened that made everything else seem even better. You know how I don't like walking in front of someone because of the whole limp problem? So I kind of waited around for Lindsey to walk first. She was waiting for me, though. Then she asked if anything was wrong, and I actually TOLD her why I get embarrassed about walking. My heart was pounding. I mean, like, going-up-a-mile-long-hill pounding. I didn't know what she would do or say. Tad told me a story a few weeks ago about how a girl he liked called him out about his limp in sixth grade, and then he stopped even trying to get out of his wheelchair at school.

You know what Lindsey did? She asked me a million questions about my leg: how it feels, when it started, whether it will ever get better, why it doesn't bother me when I'm on my bike. Then she said, "Thanks for talking with me about it. I was afraid to ask. I didn't want you to think I was shallow, but I wanted to know. I want to know everything about you."

I can't believe how this girl is always three steps more mature than me, in every single possible way. Did you ever feel like that with Annette? That somehow, while you'd been learning how to incinerate bugs with a magnifying glass and make fart noises with your armpit, she'd taken some secret girl class that made her an expert on guys? I mean, I could never think Lindsey was shallow. Seriously, if I'm a puddle, she's the Pacific Ocean. But I didn't say that to her. All I could get out was, "Uh, no problem."

She looked at me like I was a cute kitten that had somehow wound up lost in her sock drawer, got up from the bench again, and held her hand out to me. We held hands — I mean, through mittens and gloves, but still — all the way home.

Thank God I'm not sending this, by the way. I could never actually tell you all this stuff, but I have to at least write it out. Obviously, I couldn't tell Tad, because I'd be getting all dorky and misty-eyed about Lindsey, and he'd be all, "Get . . . me . . . a . . . bucket! Must . . . spew!"

So who else is there? Mom? Yeah, that would be a comfortable and useful chat. Or Dad? Can you imagine? "Uh, Dad, did you ever feel like you and Mom were, like, destined to meet?" "Well, son, there are a lot of variables that determine who we meet. For example, where we were born. If there are, say, thirty thousand towns in America alone, and each has, on average, five thousand adolescents of each gender . . . but wait — you have to factor in that the vast majority marry partners who are within just a few years of their age. Hmm . . . and then some percentage of the population moves at least once every few years. Tell you what, Jeff — I can write an equation for this, if you'd like. Does that sound like fun?"

Nah, I'd rather go flatten my tongue with a steam iron.

Anyway, that was Christmas with Lindsey. Meanwhile, Tad has still been completely strange. Usually, he's slightly nice to me, but horrible to everyone else. This week, after he got in trouble with Miss Palma (remember — the only freaking person you ever e-mail?), he decided that he is going to be kind to everyone.

Except me. And I have no idea what I did wrong.

Meanwhile, I haven't mentioned the worst thing of all. We took a pretest for the statewide math test right before vacation, and I'm pretty sure I failed it. Tad asked me how I did, and I gave him a little thumbs-up sign. Lindsey asked, too, and I changed the subject. Mom and Dad asked, and I screamed and yelled at them to trust me, for a change. Truthfully, I felt like I was being kind of harsh, but I'd rather get in trouble for having an attitude than for having brain damage (long story).

So over this whole break, even while I was opening presents, or all cozied up with Lindsey, the pretest has been rattling around in the pit of my stomach. If I did fail this thing, all H-E-double-hockey-sticks is going to break loose.

Usually when I write one of these pretend letters to you, my big hope is that you'll come home and we can be brothers again. But right now, I'd be kind of cool with just fleeing to Africa to hang out with you for a while. I'd miss Lindsey, but hey — maybe she could visit me and we could ride a llama together or something.

Or a yak. Does either one of those live in Africa?

All right, gotta go read for English. When you had Miss Palma, was she totally in love with a really hard play called *Cyrano de Bergerac*? Don't tell anybody, but it's kind of good.

Your brother,

Jeff

So that was my holiday week. The only part I didn't put in there was all the stuff about how stupid and helpless Mom thinks I am, or how Dad thinks I could just shrug off my math problem if I tried a little harder. Oh, I also left out all the times I begged them to let me go to Lindsey's house or meet her somewhere. We talked on the phone for millions of hours, but that's not the same as being together.

Can you believe I was psyched to get back to school?

At least until I got there. On the first day back, Dr. Galley called me downstairs again. There was a girl walking out of her office in tears, holding a fistful of candy hearts, which didn't seem like a good omen.

When I got in there, Dr. Galley was refilling her little glass dish from a huge industrial-size bag of hearts — also not a sign of good fortune. She started me off with small talk about my Christmas, but before I could even finish pretending to be excited about my presents, she shoved the little dish my way.

The pretest scores were back. I had failed, big-time. Now I would have to attend a special extra math class on Tuesdays and Wednesdays after school. I asked her whether the school was really allowed to do this. I mean, I was passing all of my classes, and the length of the school day was supposed to be the same for everyone, right? She took off her bifocals and rubbed the bridge of her nose. Then she told me I had a point, but that it wasn't up to her to decide what the district could or couldn't do. "If I were a student, and I had a legitimate problem with a district policy," she said, "I would tell my parents all about the situation and let them fight it out with the superintendent's office."

"So you think I have a legitimate complaint?"

She hesitated, then nodded.

"And do you think my parents have a shot at getting me out of this class?"

"Would you like another candy heart, Jeff?"

I was totally bummed about this. Wouldn't you be? I couldn't believe I was busting my butt, and getting better grades than ever before, but I was in danger of getting held back in eighth grade AND now I had to go to these stupid remedial math classes. What were they going to teach us after school that we couldn't learn during the day? I figured all I was going to get out of this course was some extra reasons to hate math — not that I needed any.

To top it all off, Tad was absent. In fact, he was out all week, and he wasn't answering IMs or e-mail. His cell phone wasn't even turned on. The message said he was out of town, and when I finally broke down and called his home number, his dad told me he was down in Philadelphia for tests. My heart skipped for a minute, but then Tad's father went on to say that everything was fine, they were just monitoring Tad's med dosages, checking his bone density, blah, blah, blah. This had happened a bunch of times before, so that seemed pretty normal.

Tad usually told me before these little trips, though.

At lunch on Wednesday that week, Lindsey asked me if I wanted to come to her house and hang out after dinner. I said I couldn't, because I was still grounded. If anything, I was even more grounded now that my parents knew about the pretest. The school had mailed a letter home, and called, AND given every student who'd failed a sign-up form that the parents had to fill out by the end of the week. It was amazing: I was almost surprised they hadn't sent singing telegrams or smoke signals.

I had never seen the school having such a major cow about anything before.

Anyway, Lindsey said, "So you still aren't allowed to go anywhere, huh? That's too bad, because my mom and my big brother are going to be out shopping for hours, and my dad's editing a film on deadline, so he won't be leaving his office in the basement all night. I'm going to be so lonely! Can't you ask?"

"There's just no way. I'm only allowed to go to Tad's." *Wait a minute*, I thought. *I'm only allowed to go to Tad's. But Mom doesn't know Tad's in Philadelphia.*

"Pretty please?" Lindsey asked. "For me?"

I remember once, when I was in my last year of treatment, I saw a poster in the bookstore that said, LIVE EVERY DAY AS THOUGH IT WERE YOUR LAST. That became sort of my unofficial motto. I mean, there was a pretty good chance I was going to die at that point, so why not live it up a little? The problem was, there isn't that much a seven-year-old can do to live it up. Fortunately, as an eighth grader with a girlfriend, my situation was a little different.

Plus, my parents were expecting me to go out to Tad's that night anyway. I wouldn't even have to lie, exactly — just take my bike and go. In the words of Miss Palma, *carpe diem*. Or, *hakuna matata*. I always get those two confused.

I smiled at Lindsey. "I'll see what I can do," I said.

What I did was flee my house after dinner like it was on fire and I was wearing a backpack full of propane. My mom asked me if I was going to Tad's, and I nodded a little. She smiled and said, "Learn a lot, OK?"

I smiled back, even though my lips suddenly felt like they were made of rubber, and I was on my bike before she could make me lie even more. I told myself it wasn't totally lying, but that was a lie, too.

It was enough to make my head hurt, but by the time I got to Lindsey's, I felt fine. Almost.

THIS CHAPTER IS PRIVATE — KEEP OUT!

Guess what? Lindsey has a sprig of mistletoe over her bedroom door.

Just sayin'.

TAD AND LINDSEY, PART 1

Tad was back in school the second week after Christmas. I asked about his trip to Philly, but he didn't want to talk about it. I understood that. If I never saw the inside of Children's Hospital again, I would still be seeing it in my nightmares forever. I could only imagine what Tad went through every time he had to go there and get poked, prodded, and stabbed.

So I said, "All your parts working OK?"

He said, "Absolutely, D.A. Just ask your mom."

And we moved on to other subjects.

My after-school math classes started that week. Incredibly, the instructor was Mr. McGrath. You know, because when mathematics is the game, and children's futures are on the line, it definitely makes sense to call in . . . THE GYM TEACHER! When I told Tad, he said, "What — there wasn't a lunch lady available?" But actually, it appeared that ol' Flash knew his stuff.

He started us off with one of his patented lame-o speeches about *vic*-to-ry, but once we got into crunching through problems, things went fine. Except for the fact that it was a whole extra freaking hour of math twice a week, that is.

Oh, there was one other problem: As you might expect from a guy named Flash, Mr. McGrath was into making us do everything as fast as possible. If you took too long on a problem, he came over and started yelling in your ear, "This is a *pow*-er test, ladies and gents — a *pow*-er test. Knowing the *an*-swers isn't enough — you have to grind it out as *fast* as you can. So we're going to drill, and drill, and drill some more until you don't have to *think* at all. Write this down: *Think*-ing is the enemy of math!"

Uh, whatever you say, Flasheroo.

After the seventeenth time he shouted at me about it, I tried to explain to him about my processing problem, my 504 plan, and how I get extra time on tests. Which was like explaining poetry to a brick wall.

"Alper," he barked, "I've been watching you all year."

I gulped. "Uh, you have?"

"Abso-*lute*-ly. You think I don't see you, just because you're in that back room? Well, that's where you're wrong. *Dead* wrong. When they put you in my class, and told me that you'd be using the *train*-ing center, I was one *hun*-dred percent against it. I thought, *Those ma*-chines *are for athletes, not for little wimps who refuse to participate in their real gym class.* But I had no choice, so I just decided I'd stay away from there, and see what happened."

He paused and stared at me from about a foot away while I resisted the urge to wipe his spit spray off my face.

"And do you know what I've seen in there this year, Alper?"

Uh, my butt? I thought. But all I said was "No, sir."

"I've seen courage. Guts. De-*ter*-mination. Why, you've taken that Ibsen boy, and you've gotten him up and out of that wheelchair. I swear, if you had told me in Sep-*tem*-ber that Ibsen would be up on the treadmill by Christmas, I'd have laughed in your face. And I've seen your workouts, too. You're *sweating* over there. You're getting stronger every day. I'm proud to say I was wrong about you, son. Now, if you can get that flabby pos-*tee*-rior of yours in shape and get your stubborn friend to walk, don't you think you can pass some namby-pamby math test?"

"Um, maybe?"

"Alper, listen: I was a track-and-field star back in the day, and my old coach told me something very important. He said, 'There's no such thing as a maybe-finish line. There's no such thing as an almost-finish line. All there is is a finish line.' Do you get my *meee*-ning?"

"I should work hard and pass the test?"

He grinned so big I could practically count the greasy chunks of Big Mac caught in his molars. "See, Alper? I knew you weren't as dumb as that big ol' five-oh-four plan said you were."

Charming guy, that McGrath. But by the time he sent me home with a CD of math flash card software and orders to practice the drills until I could do them in my sleep, he almost had me be-*lee*-ving I could pass the test.

On the way home, since I was out and about anyway and my parents were at work, I almost rode my bike over to Lindsey's. But then I thought maybe it wouldn't be such a bad idea to try the math practice program, so I went straight home. I ate some popcorn as soon as I walked in, but then I pretty much went straight to my room, fired up the computer, and worked on math speed drills until my head was spinning.

It's strange. My father had been bugging me about practicing with flash cards for years, but I always thought he was just being mean and bossy. Then, as soon as my gym teacher gave me a pep talk and told me to work on those same exact facts — even though he actually *was* kind of mean and bossy — I ran home and did it. But, you know, he wasn't my dad.

When my parents came home, they had a million questions about my after-school class. I told them the basics, but didn't mention my special moment with Flash McGrath. I don't know why. Then Mom asked if I had seen Tad around school, and how he seemed. I told her he was fine, and she exchanged some kind of mysterious look with my dad. "What?" I said. "Nothing, Jeffrey," she replied. "Aren't I allowed to look at my handsome husband once in a while?"

Thanks for saying that, Mother. It didn't make me too uncomfortable.

Luckily, Lindsey called me right then, which allowed me to flee to my room. I swear, if my parents had started kissing or something, I would have had to rip my own eyes out of my head to make the pain stop.

The next Monday I said something I shouldn't have. I was talking with Lindsey during a science lab. We were measuring water, then boiling it for a while, then measuring it again, then boiling it again, et cetera. Lindsey was the boiling-and-measuring person, and I was the timer. Again.

I don't know why the spacey kid is always the

timer. And then Mr. Laurenzano wonders why our results don't make sense.

But anyway, the boiling took a few minutes each time, so we had long stretches with nothing to do. Lindsey was filling me in on what was going on with her friends back in California. To tell you the truth, I couldn't keep all the Tiffanys and Alexises straight from the Ferns and Topangas, but I tried really hard to nod at the right times.

I must have messed up, though, because all of a sudden, Lindsey was stomping her foot and looking mad, but I had no idea what we were discussing. "Isn't that, like, so wrong?" she asked.

"Oh, yeah. It's, like, super-wrong. Ultra-wrong, even."

Then she laughed. "I just told you that Brittany-with-a-y has a cat, and it just had new kittens. I knew you weren't listening, you big goofball!"

I don't know how she can stand me sometimes. She just shrugged it off and continued, though. "No, really, I did get a little upset about one thing that happened. Remember I told you about Brittanie-with-an-*i-e*, and her ecology project?"

"Uh, maybe?" I said hopefully.

She elbowed me in the gut, but smiled so I knew it wasn't an angry elbowing. "She's the one who watched the toads in the pond on that vacant lot? And that company was going to build six hundred condos right over the pond?"

"I totally knew that, Linds."

She snorted. "Anyway — ooh, the water is boiling! Quick, write down the time!"

While I was writing and she was measuring, she said, "Well, it turns out that those toads are endangered, and that the pond qualifies as a protected wetland. And Brittanie-with-an-*i-e*'s dad is this high-powered lawyer. So he filed an injunction at the county courthouse, and now the developers can't build anything there! She's, like, an environmentalist hero. Oops, watch that burner!"

"Yikes!" I said, yanking my sleeve away from the open flame.

"So I was thinking about it, and I just got a little bummed."

"Wait, I'm confused. *Why* are you bummed again? Are you, like, anti-frog or something?"

She rolled her eyes. "No, I'm not anti-frog. And they're toads, anyway. It's just that Brittanie did something big. She turned a school project into something that really made a difference in the world. I wish I could do that. I have this project due in May for Mrs. Delpriore's English class — I'm supposed to make a video documentary on an issue that matters to me. I want to make it important, you know?"

Mr. Laurenzano said, "Lindsey, that is a splendid ambition." Geez, don't you hate it when teachers sneak up on you? "That is, if you and Jeffrey manage to survive this experiment without setting your-selves or anyone else on fire."

"No problem," Lindsey said. "Stop, drop, and roll, right?"

If a boy had said that, Mr. L. would have proba-bly launched into a big safety lecture. But he just gave that little teacher-pretending-he-isn't-really-amused-by-a-student's-joke chuckle and moved on to harass somebody else.

As soon as he was a table away, I made my big mistake. "Lindsey," I said, "you sound just like Tad."

"I do?"

"Yeah. A couple of weeks ago we had this whole big argument, because he wants to come up with some kind of grand gesture that nobody will ever forget. I told him he should just be nice, and it hurt his feelings. But the point is, Tad wants to do something important, too. Maybe you guys could — I don't know — save a tree or something."

Look, it was just an innocent comment, OK? I was just attempting to show some support for my girlfriend, and maybe trying to show her that Tad cared about more than just trading insults with people. I had no idea they were going to go off on some massive holy crusade or anything.

But as soon as I said that, Lindsey started staring off into space with a disturbing gleam in her eye. In fact, if our water hadn't boiled over onto my lab notebook at that exact moment, she might *still* be in the lab, brainstorming ways that she and Tad could turn my whole life upside down. But it did, and she got distracted for twenty-five whole hours, until she and Tad sat down for lunch the next day.

And began to make plans.

TAD AND LINDSEY, PART ii

When I got home from school, the day of the boiling-water lab, I didn't feel quite right. It got worse after dinner, and by seven o'clock, I was violently sick to my stomach in the bathroom. Repeatedly. Now, one thing you have to understand about cancer survivors is that we have a lot of experience with, shall we say, reverse digestion. The people around us might get all flipped out about it, but pretty much any illness I get isn't a big deal compared to what I've already been through.

That's why I was calm, even when the fever and shakes started at around nine. Mom, on the other hand, was about as calm as Bambi after the forest fire. So, believe it or not, she took me to the emergency room. My dad stood in the doorway, gave me an awkward pat on the shoulder as we headed for the car, and waved stiffly from the porch until Mom and I turned the corner. Mom was sporting ragged sweatpants, some kind of horrendous do-rag on her head, and the ancient tie-dye T-shirt that she slept in when her *good* ancient tie-dye T-shirt was in the wash.

As we pulled over on the highway for the second time in a mile so I could hurl in a hedgerow, I thought, *Wow, this is just like old times. Except back in the day, Steven would have been around to tell me I was going to be OK.*

And then I thought, *I don't need Steven to tell me that anymore. I know I'm OK.*

Huh, how about that? It's not often you have a major life-changing realization right in the middle of feeding the highway department's hydrangeas. Eventually I got back in the car, we made it to the hospital, and I spent the rest of the night having all sorts of unpleasantly familiar blood work. At about six AM, when my fever had broken and I was passed out on an exam-room bed, my pediatrician, Dr. Purow, came in to tell me that — surprise — I was fine. It was just a stomach bug.

Mom got all teary-eyed and hugged me, right in front of Dr. Purow. Sheesh, like this whole scene hadn't happened every time I had a fever for the past eight years. Then she asked how many days of school I would have to miss. He told her the usual: no school until at least twenty-four hours after my fever went away.

And that's why Lindsey and Tad got to have lunch alone together, head-to-head, conspiring against me, for the next three days. For the first day, I mostly slept. My biggest adventure was in the afternoon, when I staggered downstairs to eat a plain cracker, which made me super-sick all over again. On the second day, between frantic phone calls from my mom ordering me to keep sipping Gatorade every twelve seconds, I spent a couple of hours doing math on the computer. Then I IM'd back and forth with Lindsey for a while:

LFromCali:	Hi. Miss U.
Dangerous_pie:	Me 2.
LFromCali:	Howya feelin'?
Dangerous_pie:	Still N2G. No school tmw.
LFromCali:	2 bad. T misses U 2.

Dangerous_pie:	T? T who?
LFromCali:	Tad, of course.
Dangerous_pie:	He hasn't checked in.
LFromCali:	Yes. Asks me every day.
Dangerous_pie:	Y not check in w/me?
LFromCali:	IDK. U call him?
Dangerous_pie:	He's not the sick 1.
LFromCali:	Hm. Grumpy much?
Dangerous_pie:	Bored. The highlight of my day was my lunch. Blue Gatorade. Woot.
LFromCali:	Aww. Did U practice math? T wants 2 know.
Dangerous_pie:	Then he can ask. But yeah. Y?
LFromCali:	U have 2 pass. What would I do in HS w/o U?
Dangerous_pie:	Nervous breakdown?
LFromCali:	Ha. U need 2 B there 2 protect me from the HS boys.
Dangerous_pie:	But then I'll be a HS boy.
LFromCali:	My HS boy. Different.
Dangerous_pie:	☺ I'm practicing.

LFromCali:	Good. BTW, I know a secret.
Dangerous_pie:	What?
LFromCali:	T + a girl.
Dangerous_pie:	???
LFromCali:	BS
Dangerous_pie:	What did I say?
LFromCali:	No, her initials are BS. Brianna Slack.
Dangerous_pie:	!!! How? She hates him.
LFromCali:	They aren't going out or anything. But remember that whole thing U told me about her asking him all about his walking? That's exactly what I did w/U. So I told him she must have liked him.
Dangerous_pie:	2 yrs ago!
LFromCali:	I know. But he has decided 2 be nice 2 her + see what happens.
Dangerous_pie:	Wow. I can't turn my back on that kid 4 1 minute.
LFromCali:	☺ G2G. Mom wants me.

| Dangerous_pie: | Bye. |
| LFromCali: | L8r. |

On the third day, after school, I got a long e-mail from Tad. Life was just getting more and more interesting.

TO: dangerous_pie@jerseynet.com
FROM: nevr_sarcastic@jerseynet.com

Hey D.A. —

Lindsey tells me you've been projectile vomiting for days on end. Sorry to hear it. I would have gotten in touch sooner, but I was too busy listening to your really bad advice. Oh, and your girlfriend's, too. Because you've given me such massive quantities of bad advice over the years, perhaps I should be more specific: I am referring to this ridiculous "be nice" thing. And Lindsey's "Brianna Slack Attack Plan: Phases 1–3."

I have been trying to score points with Brianna for two days now, and so far the score is Humiliation: 3, Tad: 0. Yesterday, I got up my nerve as she was putting condiments on her sandwich at lunch. I wheeled my way over, cleared my throat, picked up the ketchup bottle, and said, *Hey, Brianna, do you want some ketchup?* Unfortunately, I couldn't see her sandwich from my angle. She gave me the kind of look usually reserved for use against, say, a gigantic sea slug that's swallowing one's toes, and said, *Sure, Tad. That* is *your name, right? I always put ketchup on my Italian hoagies. Dork!*

Then she walked away in a huff. If it's possible to slink in a wheelchair, I slunk back to our table, where Lindsey was dying to know what happened. *Brianna's totally hot for me,* I said. *Although admittedly, she's hiding it pretty well.*

Lindsey was all *Be patient, Rome wasn't built in a day.* Which wasn't exactly what I wanted to hear at that exact moment. Plus, who actually *says* that anyway?

Anyway, L. convinced me to try again later on. So on the way out of gym, I made sure I was behind Brianna. I was trying to think of an excuse to talk to her, when she whirled around and said, *What are you doing?* I said, *What do you mean?* She said, *You're, like, stalking me.* I said, *What? It's a public hallway.* She said, *Yeah, but you haven't been within ten feet of me since sixth grade and now you come up to me twice in a day. What are the odds?* Then she stormed into the stairwell, and I once again wheel-slunk away.

I don't remember Brianna being this tough in sixth grade. Do you?

Yeah, yeah, I called her Zitzilla. But isn't an otherwise charming guy like me allowed one slip of the tongue over the entire course of a relationship? Needless to say, Lindsey told me this morning that I should try again. According to L.'s warped thinking, Brianna's angry reactions show how much she cares.

You know, deep down.

So I gave it one more shot today in English class. We were talking about Cyrano. (By the way, read Act V and write a response journal for tomorrow. OR whenever you get your head out of the bucket.) Miss Palma asked whether we felt people deserve a second chance in life. Here's the little dialogue that followed:

Brianna: I think people definitely deserve a sec-
             ond chance.
Me: I agree. Brianna is 100 percent right.

Brianna: Unless they're sleazy, insulting idiots.

Me: Which they aren't.

Brianna: (*Snort*)

Me: No, I'm serious. What if a certain person just said one thing in anger? Are they supposed to be an outcast forever, just because of one moment of weakness?

Brianna: Totally. Especially if they're, like, famous for saying mean things anyway. My mom always says, *Fool me once, shame on you. Fool me twice, shame on me.* So why give a serial insulter another chance to strike?

Me: Oh, like the insulter just insulted the insultee for no reason at all? It was just a random act of, um, insultment?

Brianna: No, apparently the insulter did it just for fun. And THEN, to top it all off, this person didn't apologize for two YEARS.

Me: Maybe he, or SHE, should have said something sooner. But maybe he, or SHE, didn't know how.

Brianna:	He doesn't usually seem to be at a loss for words.
Me:	(*Takes deep breath*) Well, he's sorry now.
Brianna:	Not accepted.
Miss Palma:	Um, does anyone else have a feeling we're not exactly talking about Cyrano anymore?

So that's it. Three strikes and I'm out. Like I even care what old Zitzilla thinks anyway. Although I must admit, her complexion has cleared up remarkably. And she does look rather fetching when she's furious.

Your nice friend,

Tad

PS — I know the throwing-up thing is rough. Keep your chin up, old boy. Unless that causes you to choke to death.

THE ENEMY OF MATH

Needless to say, I didn't choke to death. Instead, I staggered back into school on Friday and got swarmed by well-wishers. I guess if everyone remembers you as the town's leukemia poster child, it only takes a three-day absence for the populace to start planning the spaghetti socials and car washes all over again. Tad snickered about "Little Saint Jeffrey's Return to Homeroom" until I said, "People would worry about you, too."

He said, "No, they wouldn't. When I was absent for the whole week, I came back and found a FOR RENT sign on the back of my seat. You're the chosen one, Jeff." He sounded just like Steven. Swell. You can never have too many people who resent you.

When we got to gym, Tad could barely make it onto the treadmill, and managed only maybe a minute at one mile per hour before he hit the big, red EMERGENCY STOP button. "Dude, are you OK?" I asked as he collapsed back into his chair.

"Totally . . . fine," he wheezed. "Just . . . a . . . little . . . winded."

Yeah, and Bill Gates is a little rich. I figured Tad had goofed off during his week in the hospital, and then again while I'd been out. Well, that would have to stop ASAP. I didn't want to nag, especially with how touchy he'd been lately, so I just said, "I guess we'll take it easy today, but you have to promise to train harder tomorrow. I heard a rumor that Brianna likes guys with really ripped quads."

"So does your —" he said, then stopped to catch his breath. Wow, this wasn't good. Tad had never been too tired to insult my mother before.

I walked over and put my hand on Tad's shoulder. "Hey, what's wrong?" I asked.

"Nothing," he insisted. "Nothing a little quality time with your mom wouldn't fix."

That was a little more like it. By the time I was done with my free weights, Tad seemed totally fine. Then after the bell rang, he wheeled out to the hallway at top speed. "Places to go, people to see," he said. "Don't wait up, OK?" For a second, I wasn't sure why he'd be in such a rush, and then I remembered: Brianna.

For the next couple of weeks, Tad gradually got his strength back. Meanwhile, I kept going to my after-school classes AND getting tutored. Tad helped me to catch up on the three days of lessons I'd missed, which was a plus, because we had a math midterm at the end of January and I got an eighty-three on it. I never mentioned to him that I'd used our tutoring time to visit Lindsey, and he never told me that he and Lindsey had a little conspiracy of their own going on.

All the while, Tad continued to be nice to Brianna, and she continued to treat him like most people treat toe fungus. But at least Tad and I were getting along OK for a while. Things didn't start to fall apart until Mr. McGrath gave yet another pretest for the statewide math exam.

Did you ever take a test and think you totally aced it but then get it back and realize it had totally aced *you*? Well, I thought I had absolutely rocked this thing — I even finished all of the sections early.

We spent two whole sessions on it, and then it took Mr. McGrath another week to grade our work. So for two weeks I walked around feeling like the King of Math. I even bragged to Tad and my parents about my newfound speed.

Imagine my surprise when Flash told me I'd flunked. He did it in the worst possible way, too. He made a big speech about how "Some of us just need a little extra push to achieve *vic*-tory, but others need a rocket strapped to their butts!" Then he gave back everyone else's tests, and called me into the hallway for a private chat.

"Alper," he said, "I've got some good news and some bad news."

"Uh, I scored so high you broke your slide rule calculating my grade?"

"Funny, but no. The good news is that you're *def*-initely working faster than before."

"So what's the bad news?"

"Let's just say that if I ever need someone who knows how to make a lot of mistakes really fast, you'll be getting the call. Didn't you think at *all* while you were taking the test?"

My head was spinning. "No, but you said that thinking is the enemy of math."

"Hmm, did I?"

I nodded weakly.

"Well, geez, what do *I* know? I'm not even a math teacher!"

I was in a terrible mood when I got home. All I kept thinking about was what Lindsey had said about her and the high school boys. I know I should have been worrying about spending another year in eighth grade, or my father disowning me, or how many enemies Tad would make in high school without me there to run interference for him. But instead I just kept picturing Lindsey surrounded by an army of guys: Jocks. Studs. Geniuses. Older guys with money, confidence, maybe even *cars*.

I was sure she'd be totally happy to just tell them, "No, thanks, I'm seeing this really cool half-wit who's repeating eighth grade."

I just wished I could talk to Steven about everything. For the first time all year, I went into his room. I'd never really noticed before how much of his stuff was from his eighth-grade year, my kindergarten year, when I was first diagnosed. There were his two favorite pairs of drumsticks: the autographed ones I'd kind of ruined that summer before school started by stirring a big old vat of raw meat with them, and the ones that he'd given to Samantha, that girl who'd been a patient on my floor in the hospital and died of leukemia. There was the poster for his first All-City jazz band concert, the one that he'd had to leave during intermission because I got a fever. And there, pinned to his bulletin board, was a picture of me and Steven on his eighth-grade graduation day. With one hand, he was holding his mortarboard cap over his head, and with the other, he was tipping my baseball cap. Our heads were mostly shaded, but you could still make out how short our hair was. Mine was just starting to grow back after chemo, and he had shaved all of his off so I wouldn't have to go through being bald all by myself.

Amazing how much of his life I'd messed up.

When I heard my mom tromping around downstairs, I hurried out of Steven's room and headed down for dinner. I swear, I was planning to tell my parents about my failing grade on the pretest, but right when I was building up my nerve, my dad launched into a whole big round of congratulations about my eighty-three on the midterm. He looked so happy about it that I just couldn't stand to destroy the moment. I figured he'd have the whole next year to suffer over my stupidity.

I went up to bed early, but had some trouble falling asleep. Every time I closed my eyes, I kept picturing Lindsey and all those high school guys. Plus, it gradually dawned on me that I could hear raised voices from downstairs. I tried to ignore them for a while, but eventually I gave up, sighed, and dragged myself over to the closet. Their conversation was yet another eye-opener.

"Look," Dad said, "it's bad enough we're not telling Jeff about the other thing. But now you go and write letters to everyone in the world to get him excused from the test?"

"It wasn't everyone in the world. At first, I tried the principal. He sent me to the superintendent. The superintendent told me to take it up with the state department of education, so that's what I did. Plus, this wasn't just about getting Jeffrey excused completely. They aren't even going to give him extra time or a small-group testing site. He's going to be right in the middle of three hundred kids in the gym, trying to concentrate and crank out the work — with no computer. I'm sorry you don't think we should advocate for our child, though."

"Advocate? *Advocate?* Is that what you call it? Because I call it 'enabling,' as in, 'you are enabling your child to remain an infant.' You saw Jeff's grade on that midterm. He can *do* this!"

Mom fired right back: "I'm telling you — AGAIN — a classroom math test is a million years removed from the statewides. It's like seeing your kid get a hit in T-ball, and saying he's ready for the major leagues. Besides which, I'm not saying he should be excused from taking the test — just from being held back if he fails. In education, we call that 'protection from adverse consequences.' It's considered an essential characteristic of a quality learning environment."

"Well, in the business world, we call that 'babying the worker,' and it's considered an essential characteristic of a poorly run company."

"Honey, I don't want to baby Jeffrey. Really, I don't. I just want him to have a chance."

"Then maybe we should be getting him a professional tutor," my dad said.

"You know we don't have that kind of money, especially now that the rate is going up on the second mortgage. And don't start in again about how we could have paid back the insurance company faster if I'd gone back to work sooner. That was years ago."

Holy cow. My parents had taken out a second mortgage on our house?

"Whatever. All I'm saying is, if you really want him to get through this, a pro is probably more effective than some gym teacher. Or Tad. Especially *now*."

Especially *now*? Why does everybody I know always seem to be speaking in code?

"You're a pro. If you're so stuck on this, why don't you work on Jeffrey's math with him?"

My dad sighed. "You know how much I'd love to do that. But Jeffrey doesn't listen to me. He never has. You know what? Maybe we should just fly Steven back from Africa once a week. Jeff listens to him like everything he says came down from a mountain carved on two clay tablets."

Whoa. Did my dad actually sound *jealous* of my brother?

"Jeffrey loves you, too, you know that."

"Not enough to let me anywhere near his math homework."

I felt sick to my stomach. All this time, I'd thought my father was so disappointed in me that working with me disgusted him. But the worst thing was that Dad was right: I *had* always liked Steven better.

At lunch the next day I told Tad about the pretest, and of course he got really upset about it. "Jeff," he said, "there's only one thing to do."

"What's that?"

"I'm gonna have to tutor you twice a week."

"Tad, I'm already going to the extra classes every Tuesday and Wednesday, plus I have math every single day, AND you've been helping me once a week since October. Do you really think another hour and a half will make a difference?"

Tad picked at his food, looking at it as though it might bite him. "I don't know, but what's the other option?"

"Well, my mom is trying to get the state to excuse me."

He nodded. "I know," he said.

"You know? How?"

He stopped looking nauseated for a moment — long enough to flash the famous Tad Ibsen smirk. "Uh, your mother and I have always been close."

"No, I'm serious. I didn't even know about this until last night, so how do you —"

"I'm sorry, Jeff, but I can't tell you. I promised someone."

"Someone?"

Just then, Lindsey banged her tray down next to mine. I jumped.

"Hi, guys!" she chirped. At least one person at this table was having a good day. "What are we promising?"

"Nothing," I mumbled.

Out of the corner of my eye, I saw Tad make a frantic throat-cutting signal to Lindsey as he said, "Nothing."

Lindsey's eyes widened. "Oh," she said quietly. "Oh."

I couldn't believe this. Whatever was going on, Lindsey was in on it, too.

THE REAL ENEMY OF MATH

You know what? Thinking isn't the enemy of math. Methotrexate is. I tried so freaking hard the next month that I thought my brain would explode, but numbers and stuff just don't stay in my head right. I had a feeling Tad was pretty frustrated, too.

Halfway through our fifth twice-a-week session, in the middle of checking my work on a word problem, he sighed and pushed my laptop away. "Let's take a break," he said. "YVONNE!" he bellowed. Tad's sister came charging into the room, pigtails flying in every direction. "Do you want some milk and cookies?" he asked her. She nodded. "Well, what are you waiting for? Go get them and bring them here!" She scampered out.

"Tad, why are you always so mean to her?"

"What do you mean?"

"Stop it. I'm serious. You're on her all the time. Why?"

"Do you really want to know?"

I nodded.

"Truthfully, I always figured I'd probably die. And I thought, *Maybe it will be easier for everyone if Yvonne doesn't get too attached to me.*"

"So you were being *nice* by being mean?"

It was Tad's turn to nod.

"That's the dumbest thing I've ever heard."

"Oh, really? Like you never gave up on anything when you were in treatment? Think real, real hard. If you're not totally full of crap, I guarantee you'll come up with something."

He was right. I knew exactly what he meant. I remembered sitting in front of my math homework in fourth grade, with my head in my hands, saying to myself, *Oh, who cares about this stuff? Mrs. Hanson said if I don't know my math facts I'll be in trouble when I grow up. But what if I don't grow up?* And then I remembered closing the workbook, going downstairs to find Steven, and asking him to play checkers with me.

Still, I couldn't believe I was having this conversation. Since when had Tad become, like, my therapist? "I have no idea what you're talking about," I said.

I had a weird feeling Tad was about to smack me or something, but then Yvonne came in carrying a huge tray with organic oatmeal cookies, cups, napkins, and a carton of milk on it. We stopped talking, and wolfed down pretty much everything. When Yvonne was piling the garbage back on the tray, Tad touched her arm and said, "Thanks, Y. That was perfect." She blushed, and scurried away.

Nice to know there was hope for *one* of us to change, anyway.

Two days later, Tad was absent again. I asked Lindsey if I could come over to her house — thanks to global warming, we were having the first no-snow winter anybody could remember, which sucked for the planet, but kind of ruled for eighth-grade boys who need to get around on bikes. She argued that I should stay home and study, but I swore I would just sit at home and watch basketball on TV if she didn't let me come over. So she let me come over. For the next few weeks, Tad was in and out of school, but every time I asked whether he was all right, he got all growly. So I guess it was easier not to ask. I mean,

I hate to say this now, but I almost *hoped* he'd be out on tutoring days so I could sneak over to Lindsey's. Until the night Lindsey kicked me to the curb.

When I got to Lindsey's house, her mom let me in and led me to the basement door. "Go on down," she said. "Lindsey is just helping her father out with some editing." I basically have to turn sideways and crab-walk to get down steep staircases, but I made it down OK. Lindsey's dad was sitting on front of a huge, awesome computer monitor, and she was leaning over his shoulder. They were watching video footage of a tanker truck explosion over and over. "Lindsey," her dad said, "do you think this is, I don't know, a little drab?"

Drab? I thought. *How drab can it be? It's a freaking explosion!*

"Maybe," Lindsey said. "Here, try this." She reached over her father and did a while lot of really fast mouse clicking. Then the explosion came on again, and it was somehow much cooler. "Well?" she asked him.

"That's it, Linds! Was that a blue filter right after the flash?"

"Yup. See, this way it's like the way a person's eyes would react to a burst of bright light. You're putting the audience right *there*, you know?"

Lindsey's dad saw me then, and said, "Come on down, Jeff. Did you know your friend Lindsey is a genius?"

"Uh, sure. I mean, yes, sir. She sure is."

Lindsey's eyes flashed. "Don't knock yourself out with excitement or anything, Jeffrey Alper."

I froze up in horror. "I didn't mean — you were — the explosion was — you're awesome!"

"And don't you forget it, Jeffrey! See you, Dad!" she said, and pushed me upstairs. Her mom brought us some drinks and chips, and then left us alone in Lindsey's room. Wow, California parents were just so different. If I wanted an instant alone with Lindsey at my house, I had to take her on a freezing death-march to the park, but at Lindsey's, they just fed us and disappeared. Leaving me IN Lindsey's ROOM.

I liked it.

At least until Lindsey turned to me and said, "Jeff, we have a problem."

"Uh, we do?"

"Yes, we do. I, uh, I think maybe we shouldn't spend time together outside of school until after the statewide tests next month."

Whoa. I felt like I had just been hit by a brick. Just then, it occurred to me that the mistletoe was gone from the doorway. "What? Why? Are you breaking up with me? I don't believe this! I thought everything was going so well, and now —"

She put her hand over my lips. "Jeff, stop! I'm not breaking up with you."

"Then why —"

"I just don't want to be a distraction. If you failed the test by, like, one point because you were with me instead of practicing, it would be awful."

"You're not a distraction. I swear! I mean, you are, but I can't study all the time. Can I?"

"Maybe you should, Jeff. Just until the test is over. By then your parents will be off your case, too, and we won't have to sneak around like —"

"What do you mean, sneak around? Your mom

just poured me a glass of milk. Apparently, she noticed I was here."

"Ha-ha. We're not sneaking around *my* parents, Jeffrey."

"Well, uh . . ."

"No, NOT well, uh! I don't want to feel like we're in trouble all the time. It's not right. And Tad thinks —"

"What does Tad have to do with this?" My mind was putting together some ugly clues: the mysterious glances, the strange silences, and whatever dire secret project they'd been doing together on the nights I'd been sitting home alone. "Oh, God, are you and Tad —"

"NO!" Lindsey practically shouted. "I can't believe you'd even *think* that! Tad and I aren't anything except two people who care about you."

"But then, what's with all the secrets? Why can't you just tell me what's going on? I mean, I'm glad you care about me so much that you're dumping me, but —"

"I'm *not* dumping you! But I promised Tad, OK? I can't tell the secrets because they're not mine to tell. If you really want to know what's going on, why don't you go over there and ask him?"

I didn't care how she played it off, I still felt very much like a dumpee. "So you want me to get out?"

"I didn't say that!"

"But you want me to go to Tad's house, right? Which means getting out of this one."

"Fine, go!"

"All right, I will!"

"Good!"

I started to storm out of her room, but it's hard to storm effectively when you're limping. And then I had to come back in because I forgot to put down my milk glass.

Yeah, I know. I'm super-bad.

As I got to the doorway the second time, Lindsey said, "Jeff, you can call me anytime tonight if you need to talk after . . ."

After what? I thought. *Is Tad going to dump me, too?* I just didn't get it: She was chasing me out of the house and telling me to call her at the same time.

I hobbled out of there as fast as I could, and before I could change my mind, I was rocketing across town on my bike. I was all worked up — I felt like I was in the intermission of a really scary play. I mean, what are the chances that you'd have your first-ever romantic breakup on a night when it's not even the worst thing that's going to happen?

I got to Tad's in record time, and rang the bell. His mom came rushing to the door, and said, "Shhh!" She led me through the foyer into the dining room, where three places were set for a late dinner.

"What's going on, Mrs. Ibsen? Is Yvonne asleep or something? I just came over to see how Tad's feeling, and if maybe he was up for some tutoring."

She gave me a weird look, kind of like she pitied me. "No, Yvonne's not asleep, Jeffrey. Tad is."

I looked at my watch. It wasn't even eight o'clock yet. "*Tad's* asleep?"

"Oh, son," Tad's mother said. "Don't you remember what evenings were like when *you* were in treatment?"

In treatment? *In treatment?*

I sat down in whatever chair was closest, and Mrs. Ibsen put a hand on my shoulder. How could I have been so blind? How could I have been so totally, obliviously stupid? I wasn't going to be sneaking in a math session, because my tutor — my best friend — had relapsed. Tad had cancer again.

Thinking isn't the enemy of math. Methotrexate isn't, either. *Cancer* is.

A BIG GROWTH YEAR

When I finally got home that night, I turned on my computer. It was too late to call Lindsey, but I thought maybe she'd be online. In a rare example of perfect timing, I had gotten an e-mail just a couple of hours before, probably while I was having a breakdown at Tad's house. It was from Steven.

TO: dangerous_pie@jerseynet.com
FROM: drum_master@jerseynet.com

Hi Jeff—

I know it's been a while since we've really talked, so I wanted to check in. A really cool Brazilian girl here has one of those infinite-time wireless Internet adapters, and we've become friends, so she's letting me write to everybody on her computer.

So how are you? I was just thinking about you, because I was telling Christianna (that's her name) your whole life story. I'm teaching her as much English as I can, and she's kind of paying me back with dance lessons. She says you can't play the samba rhythm right unless you know the dance, too.

Anyway, wow! Eighth grade, and you're already almost three-quarters of the way done with it. Time has flown here because I am learning so much, but it still amazes me how old you are. I'm dying to know how life is going. My eighth-grade year wasn't perfect, but I think I discovered more about myself in those ten months than I ever had before, and probably than I have in any year since — this year comes close, though.

I hope you're having a good time, and that you're stopping to appreciate the people and things around you. I know this sounds corny, but once you get to high school, everything will be different.

If you e-mail me back within the next couple of days, I'll be able to read it before Christianna leaves camp. She's going on a three-week photo safari after that, so who knows when my next chance will be.

Say hi to Miss Palma, OK?

Steven

His next chance? His next chance for what? Never mind — I didn't want clarification. What I really wanted was to scream and yell and punch the walls. But I settled for just typing really hard.

TO: drum_master@jerseynet.com
FROM: dangerous_pie@jerseynet.com

Hi Steven —

Nice of you to drop me a line. If you can pause for a minute in your Brazilian dance party, I'll give you the update. After all, it's not every day your little bro has a nervous breakdown.

Guess who has CML? Maybe you've heard of CML — chronic myelogenous leukemia? The kind of leukemia that can only be cured by a bone marrow transplant? And it's super-rare in kids? Plus, it's even rarer in kids who've survived cancer? Well, anyway, Tad has it now. I mean, wow! What are the chances that a kid could survive one brain tumor, brain surgery, another brain tumor, chemo, brain surgery AGAIN, radiation treatments, a bone marrow transplant, and several years in a wheelchair, just to get a whole other, freakishly unusual, terminal illness at the end? The doctors say they've never seen anything like Tad's case. Isn't that special?

It's such a funny story, how he knew something was wrong for months, but didn't even tell me. Oh, and he told Lindsey — that's the girl I've been seeing — about his new diagnosis a month ago. So she didn't tell me for four weeks, and then dumped me today right before I finally stumbled upon the truth. Hey, and guess who's mad at me now? Mom and Dad, because I went on this whole crying jag with Tad's mother, so she called them to come get me. But then she mentioned I had just stopped by for the first time in a while, when I had been lying to them for weeks by saying I was going to Tad's to be tutored.

Because I'm going to fail the standardized math test and have to repeat eighth grade. Did I forget that part? And I'm grounded, too. Hence the lying, so I could sneak over to Lindsey's for a nice round of getting ditched.

I can't believe myself. I can't believe I even care about being in trouble, or the math stuff, or my stupid eighth-grade breakup issues, while Tad is in terrible shape. He already started high-intensity chemo with this one drug called Gleevec. The doctors think that if the Gleevec doesn't work, he's going to need radiation AND a bone marrow transplant. They know from last time that his little sister, Yvonne, is a match, so she's going in for some blood work tomorrow.

I can't imagine being her. What must she be thinking tonight? I know how shocked and terrified I am, and Tad isn't even my brother.

God, Steven. What was it like being *you* when I was sick?

Geez, I was furious at you three paragraphs ago, and now I almost feel sorry for you. On the one hand, I'm mad that you're not HERE. And here's a tip: I don't want to hear about your stupid samba partner when I know Annette is still in America, waiting around for you. But on the other hand, I looked at Yvonne tonight and . . . well, you know. She just looked so sad.

Oh, gotta go. Mom's knocking on the door.

Your brother,

Jeff

So my mom came in. I wasn't sure if she was going to yell, or be all huggy and supportive. I also wasn't sure which would be worse. At least with yelling, you can get all mad and defend yourself. But with the sympathy visit, you have to talk about all the horrible stuff that's going on.

As soon as I saw her face, I knew it was support time. Her eyes were all red-rimmed, and she was holding a crumpled-up, soggy-looking tissue in one hand. "Oh, Jeffy, I'm so sorry," she said.

"Why?" I said. "You didn't give Tad leukemia. Plus, I'm not mad at you. You're supposed to be mad at *me*."

"Jeff, don't get me wrong. I'm not happy that you were sneaking over to Lindsey's house when you were supposed to be studying with Tad. It was irresponsible, and an incredibly bad idea at this point in your school career. But at least that's normal kid stuff. I understand it. This cancer thing, though —"

I did *not* want Mom to talk about "this cancer thing" yet. Just hearing Mom say it made me feel like someone had just plugged my spine into an electric socket. So I went with the Lindsey angle. "Mom, can I tell you why I went to Lindsey's?"

She raised an eyebrow. "Buddy," she said, "I know *exactly* why you went to Lindsey's."

I could feel my face turning bright red. "Mom!"

She chuckled. "You don't have to explain that part to me, all right? I was a teenager once, too. And teenagers do this stuff. The only teen I know that never really rebelled is your brother. So he's doing it now."

"What are you talking about?"

She sighed. "Jeff, do you remember when you were in third grade, you had to do a report about the Amish?"

Hmm. I had some vague recollection of trying to make a black hat out of construction paper. "Uhh, yeah?"

"You might remember that the Amish people have a tradition called Rumspringa. Does that ring a bell?"

What was this woman *talking* about? This was the worst crisis of my life, and she was having flashbacks of my elementary school social studies projects. I shook my head, which was all the encouragement Mom needed to slip into teacher mode.

"See, when Amish children turn sixteen, they get to spend a year acting like regular, ordinary, modern people — what the Amish call 'the English.'"

"And?"

"The idea is, they spend a year trying out all the things that are forbidden in their culture. Then at the end of the year, they have to decide whether to give it all up and go back to living the Amish life, or leave their culture and live in our world."

I still didn't get it. "So?"

"So that's a really brilliant idea, I think. Kids need to get this stuff out of their systems. Parents agonize over it, but it's true. If you never rebel, you build up a ton of resentment. And then, when it comes out later — boom!"

Oh, now I knew where Mom was going. It's funny: I had thought of a lot of reasons why Steven had quit the world, but being insufficiently Amish wasn't one of them. "You leave your family, dump your girl-friend, and go to Africa?"

"Bingo. Your brother spent his teen years being perfect. With everything that was going on, there was just no room for him to go wild. So he started dating the most responsible girl in the world, threw himself into every worthy cause he could find, acted like the ideal big brother, and never did anything wrong at home."

"So this is all because of my cancer, right? I know I ruined Steven's life. But does he have to stay away forever?"

"You absolutely did NOT ruin Steven's life. And he'll be back," Mom said.

"Oh, yeah? What about this?" I asked. I let her read Steven's message. Not my unsent reply, though.

When she finished reading it, she said, "Don't worry. I know your brother. He'll be home by your graduation."

"But —"

"I've never seen two people as attached to each other as your brother and Annette. Trust me. He'll be back, and it will all be fine."

It must be nice to be totally delusional, I thought. I'd love to believe my brother was about to give up his wild ways, drive home from Africa in an Amish buggy, and get back to normal. I'd love to believe I could fly, too, but that doesn't mean I'm gonna go jump off a building. "Trust me," she says. Sheesh.

"Now," Mom said. "About Tad's illness."

"I don't want to talk about it."

"It isn't going to go away just because we don't talk about it, Jeffrey."

Great, I thought. NOW she's a realist.

"Mom, can I please just go to sleep?"

"All right, but I'm downstairs if you need me."

She ruffled my hair and went out. I curled up in bed and faced the wall. I don't think I actually fell asleep until about four AM, though. Steven had always been the one person who could calm me down in the middle of the night, and no matter what my mother said, he wasn't exactly available. So I lay there, hour after hour, and tried very, very hard not to think about Tad.

I figured, *Hey, if denial works for Mom, why not give it a try?*

ON THE TREADMILL

Speaking of denial, Tad and I didn't discuss his cancer for another week or so. I mean, I tried to bring it up several times, but he was all *Don't worry about it, I'll be fine. Let's study.* Or *Chill, Jeff. It's N.B.D. I'll just take my Gleevec and my prednisone, get into remission, and get a bone marrow transplant. No biggie. Now put on your big-boy pants and do another set of curls.*

I got madder and madder, but you can't make a guy talk about his cancer before he wants to. Meanwhile, Lindsey kept trying to get me to talk, but I just kept getting madder and madder at her, too. I mean, first she knew about Tad's sickness before I did, and didn't tell me, then she dumped me on the night she sent me to find out. She kept telling me it was all for my own good — because, you know, I love to be patronized and pitied at the same time. I felt like I was a racehorse with a broken leg, and she was my vet. What was she going to do next, take me out behind the barn and shoot me?

Oh, and my mom heard back from the state department of education. That's what finally blew everything wide open. The morning after I over-heard her telling my dad about the decision, I made the mistake of telling Tad about it while I was on the exercise bike.

"So then," I panted, "my father goes, 'Good. Now Jeff can stand on his own two feet and show 'em.' Then Mom goes, 'Or he can fail the test and get held back. I can't believe this is happening right now, when Jeffy has already been through so much.' Dad gets all snappy and goes, 'And another thing: Stop calling him "Jeffy." For God's sake, the kid is thirteen years old. Maybe this is the perfect time for him to prove himself.'"

"You know what, D.A.?" Tad said. "I know the test thing sucks, but I think it's kind of cool that your dad has faith in you."

"Sure. It's swell. Except I think my mom's right."

Tad said, "Stop."

"What?"

"Stop pedaling. This is important."

"Dude, I'm just hitting my pace here. I can talk fine."

"Jeff, stop. Please."

Yowza. Tad never said please. I stopped, grabbed my little sweat towel, and wiped my forehead. "OK, what's up?"

Tad looked right into my eyes in an oddly intense way and said, "Both of your parents are right. You shouldn't have to pass the stupid test to graduate. But you WILL be ready for it. All you have to do is work hard and stop with the self-doubt crap. Brother Thaddeus has a plan."

Brother Thaddeus? What the heck was *that* about? I mean, I've had cancer, too, and it didn't suddenly turn me into a monk. "What plan?"

"Can't tell you yet."

"Yeah," I muttered, "you've been big on the not-telling-me lately."

Now Tad looked annoyed. "Oh, gimme a break,

Jeff. In case you hadn't noticed, I've had more on my mind lately than whether or not I've given you your daily briefing."

"Uh, I hate to break it to you, but it's not like you forgot something minor. Forgetting to tell your best friend you have a cavity — that's minor. Forgetting to tell your best friend you have a bad hangnail — that's minor. Forgetting to tell your best friend you have freaking *leukemia* is major!"

Tad looked down and played with the right wheel of his chair. "I didn't want to tell you until after the test. You *have* to pass."

"I've been hearing that a lot lately. But I don't care — your cancer is a bigger deal than my math score."

"Whatever," Tad said. "I just . . . look, your score matters to me, OK? I just want to know you're gonna make it to high school."

Just then, I saw through the glass wall behind Tad that Flash McGrath was striding toward us. *Great*, I thought. *The one time he comes in here all year, and we're not even doing anything.* I started pedaling again.

"Uh, Tad?" I said. "We can talk more about this later, all right? I think it's time for you to get on the treadmill."

"Not doing it," he said.

"What are you talking about?"

"No point."

"No point? What about graduation? What about your big walk across that stage? Isn't that going to be, like, the biggest beau geste of all?"

"Jeff, you still don't get it. Impressing Brianna isn't my biggest beau geste. Walking fifteen feet in a gown wouldn't be my biggest beau geste." His voice dropped so low I could barely hear it over the sound of the exercise bike. "*You're* my biggest beau geste. Getting you onto that stage is way more important to me than strolling across it."

Flash was now staring in at us, but I guess because I was pedaling again, he got bored after thirty seconds or so, and turned away. I still wanted to get Tad onto his machine, though. All of a sudden, it felt like the most important thing in the world. Sometimes when you're at a huge fork in the road, you don't even realize it until later. But other times, you can feel it in your bone marrow.

"Yeah, that's very touching, Tad. Remind me to buy you some flowers later. Now get off your butt and start walking. Come on, I'll only make you do a minute today if you crank up the speed a little."

"They scheduled my transplant, Jeff. If my cancer is in remission, they're going to do it three weeks after the statewides. Then I'm going to be in isolation for at least six weeks."

I stopped pedaling. I can barely do math when I'm sitting still. "Wait, but that means —"

"I'm not going to be at graduation."

This couldn't be. It just couldn't be. "Tad," I said, "get on the treadmill. Please."

"Jeff, weren't you listening just now? There's no point. I'm going to be in a damn hospital bed on the day you —"

"I don't care! Get on the treadmill! You can't just quit on me!"

"I'm not quitting on you, I swear. It just . . . I'm pretty dizzy lately. And it hurts to walk."

"GET ON THE TREADMILL!" I shouted. "Get *on*! Get ON!" I started trying to push Tad's wheelchair across the room, but he locked the wheels. "You have to! You *have* to!"

I must have gotten pretty loud, because Flash walked into the room — and found Tad hunched over with his head in his hands, and me sitting on the floor, crying. He sent me down to Dr. Galley's office, and kept Tad for a private chat — probably the first time in history that a teacher thought Tad would be easier to handle than me. I tried to calm down on the way to the counseling office, but it was like the air was too thin or something. I just couldn't catch my breath.

The guidance secretary took about a millionth of a second to decide she didn't want any part of me, either, and practically shoved me into Dr. Galley's office. Within two seconds of my butt hitting the chair, I was wiping my nose and sucking on a candy heart at the same time. Dr. Galley was as unfazed as ever. All she said was, "Rough day at the office?"

And then I told her everything. She ignored her phone, her beeping e-mail, and even some knocks on her office door. When I was finished, she said, "May I see your application, please?"

"What are you talking about?"

"Well, you seem to feel that everything that's wrong is because of your cancer. Am I right?"

"I don't think that, I *know* it. If I hadn't had cancer, Steven wouldn't be having his stupid midlife crisis. AND I would have a normal relationship with my dad. AND my family wouldn't be poor. AND I wouldn't suck at math. Sorry, I mean 'stink.' AND I'd still have a girlfriend. AND Tad wouldn't be worrying about my stupid math when he should be worried about himself."

"OK, then I want to see your cancer application."

"Dr. Galley, I don't know what you're talking about."

"So, when you got cancer, you didn't fill out any kind of application first?"

I was baffled. I shook my head.

"You didn't write a letter to Santa asking for a lethal blood disease? You didn't go to church and pray for chemotherapy? You didn't sacrifice a goat to the Leukemia God?"

I shook my head again. What was this woman talking about?

"You know what this means?"

"Uh, you had an extra martini with lunch?"

"Jeffrey, it means your cancer wasn't your fault. Which means other people's reactions to it aren't your fault, either. And then there's Tad: Nothing you've done has anything to do with Tad's relapse."

"I didn't say my cancer was my fault."

"Not in those words, no. But look — have you ever played cards?"

"Um, yeah. When I was little, in the hospital, Steven used to play Go Fish with me all the time. And then when I got bigger, he and Annette taught me to play Hearts."

"And when the cards were dealt, did you punch yourself in the head every time you got a bad hand? Or did you just play the cards you got?"

I thought about that for so long that Dr. G. gave me another candy heart. I still wasn't sure whether she was completely bonkers, or a genius. But I felt a little better, like whatever had been clenched up in my chest had relaxed a bit.

"OK, I get it. I can't control the past. But that doesn't solve my problems. Or Tad's. What am I supposed to do if he's just giving up?"

"Support him, Jeff," Dr. Galley said. "That's all anybody can ever do. Find a way to support him." And with that, she sent me off to class. Of course, I spent the rest of the day in a fog, trying desperately to find a way to show support for Tad — the one person in the world who loathed being helped in any way. I mean, what was I supposed to do, organize a group hug in English class? Bring him daisies at lunch?

As if I didn't have enough to think about, I didn't get a chance to talk with Tad the rest of the day, and then he was out of school three days in a row while I sat and worried. When he showed up in homeroom on the fourth day, he just chattered away as though nothing had happened. But in gym, he got back on the treadmill. In fact, he was working out harder than ever.

Meanwhile, something else was going on. Kids kept coming up to me and saying, "Dude, I'm totally with you," or "I'm behind you all the way, man." I had no clue what they were talking about, but I just kind of nodded and half smiled at them. It's bad enough not knowing what the heck is going on, but it's even worse to admit it.

I should have asked somebody.

ONE SMALL STEP FOR MAN

The last few weeks before the test were a blur: of kids winking and nudging me for no apparent reason; of Lindsey squeezing my hand supportively under the table in science class, but refusing to see me outside of school; of Tad pretending everything was fine one minute, and then wheeling himself out of class at top speed to vomit the next. It was a weird time. Huge things were going wrong right and left, but nobody was discussing any of it.

And Tad looked awful. His hair was thinning, his face was all puffed up from the flattering combined effects of the chemo and the steroids, and he had random muscle cramps that made him grimace all through our tutoring sessions. But if I asked, he'd say, *N.B.D., D.A.,* and hand me another set of word problems.

Then, exactly one week before the big day, I had two inspirations. Sitting in my room listening to my parents arguing over the testing, I figured out how to make a grand gesture for my dad. That same evening, as I was falling asleep, I came up with my beau geste for Tad, too. The Dad one was easy. All I did was pick a problem from my practice workbook that I didn't understand — and believe me, it wasn't hard to find one — grab my math stuff, and walk down to the kitchen.

"Dad," I said, "can I interrupt? I'm upstairs studying, and there's this one problem I don't get. Can you help me?" My father's face lit up like I was handing him the keys to the Beemer he's always wanted, while my mother smiled warmly and disappeared from the room.

When Dad was done sharing all of his pent-up mathematical joy with me, and I was in bed, the Tad thing popped into my head. It was so simple: I would dedicate my The Moving On Bike-a-Thon to him. I don't usually like to talk about it with people, and of course Tad said it was dorky — but he always donated. Generally I asked only relatives and my family's friends to contribute, so I had never even mentioned the ride at school before, but maybe if I asked people to donate in Tad's name, he would see that a whole bunch of people supported him. I went downstairs and looked at the big family calendar that my mom keeps on the breakfast bar, and realized with a shock that the big ride was scheduled for the day after Tad's transplant procedure. Which was kind of a good thing — being out there raising money would definitely be better than just sitting around worrying the whole day.

I figured the worst thing that could happen is I'd rake in some extra bucks for the cause. So I went to sleep feeling pretty good, for a change.

The next day I brought my sign-up sheet to school and started passing it around. On the way, I'd gotten kind of crazy and decided to do fifty miles instead of twenty-five. By lunch, I had something like eighty kids signed up to chip in a dime a mile. The weird thing was how happy everybody was about this. One guy slapped me on the back and said, "Dude, tit for tat. That's so cool!" I had no idea what he was talking about, but hey — his money was just as green as everybody else's. Then in the hall before lunch,

Brianna Slack marched up to me, handed me a crumpled-up twenty-dollar bill, said, "Don't you *dare* tell him," and stormed into the cafeteria.

When I got to our table, I was the first one there. Tad wheeled up a moment later with a strange glint in his eye, and said, "So, D.A., you've finally gone and turned *me* into a poster child."

"Tad, I just wanted you to see that people care about you."

He put his hand on my arm and said, "Jeff. It's OK. Thank you." Then he looked around to make sure nobody could hear, leaned all the way close to me, and said, "So, how much did Brianna Slack give?"

And that was that.

The rest of the week seemed to go super-fast and super-slowly at the same time. All we did in every class was review, review, review, and practice, practice, practice — except in Miss Palma's class, where we did freewriting and improvisational acting exercises to "cleanse our overloaded minds." The endless flow of worksheets was torture, but it also had a strangely numbing effect. And by the time I knew it, I was walking out of the building on Friday afternoon, with nothing but a weekend between me and a date with the cruel hand of Destiny. Or, at least, the state board of education.

On the steps, Lindsey rushed up, threw her arms around me, and gave me a rather bone-crushing hug. I was totally stunned. Between the smell of her hair, the feeling of our bodies being pressed together, and the fact that we just didn't *do* this in public, it was too much for my brain to process. I stood there like one of those antique wooden Indians from a cigar store as she pushed me to arm's length and said, "Jeff, whatever happens, I can't wait until the tests are over. I can't wait to have you back."

I was still frozen.

"Uh, Jeffrey Alper? Hello?"

"Yeah. Um, right. After the test. Back. Good."

Then she said, kind of shakily, "So please don't be mad at me, all right? Everything I did was for you. Please know that."

"Uh, good. For me. Thanks!"

She tilted her head as though if she angled her ears differently, she would suddenly be able to interpret my strange caveman dialect. Then she squeezed my left arm one more time, and ran down the stairs to her mom's car.

What did she mean, *everything* she did? All I knew about was the temporary dumping. Was there more? It's amazing how many times a day I am totally baffled by the people around me.

I went home to the longest weekend of my life. The first day of the testing was a new science section that didn't even count, but I still spent Friday, Saturday, and Sunday nights sweating through my covers over and over again. I kept having these crazy dreams:

- I'm chained to the wall of a dark, shadowy testing dungeon. I can tell that's what it is because there's a big torchlit sign on the opposite wall, next to the electric pencil sharpener. A hooded torturer with a familiar voice says, "Well, Alper, now your butt is in a pile of trouble! Only five *min*-utes left, and you still haven't even started! Why don't you get that *hi*-ney down from there, and start bubbling in some *an*-swers?" "But, sir," I cry in anguish, "I'm handcuffed to the wall!" I shake my arm and leg irons at him and add, "Can't you undo these?" "Sorry," he says, "I'm only a gym teacher!"

• We're in the school gym, which is the actual testing site. But in the dream version, there are weird scientific devices hanging down from the ceiling where the climbing ropes should be. Lindsey is there. She raises her hand and asks for a new number two pencil. The hair on the back of my arms stands up, and then a bolt of lightning crashes down and completely obliterates her. The kid to my left murmurs, "Harsh, dude. Harsh."

• I'm in the gym again, but this time it's decked out like the Death Star from an old *Star Wars* movie. The whole eighth grade is sitting at regular school desks, but we all have strange robes on, and some kids have green faces and/or antennae. I'm trying to use a calculator that's shaped like the handle of a lightsaber.

The ghostly form of Tad appears floating in the air before me. "Turn off the computer, Jeffrey. Use the Force. Reach out with your feelings!" I start to put down the calculator, but accidentally push the wrong button. The blade comes flashing to life, and cuts a massive hole in both my desk and my right leg. That same kid from the other dream is still next to me, but now he's wearing a stormtrooper helmet. "Oh, man," he says. "*That's* gonna cost you some points!"

By the time Monday came, I was almost relieved to head into the gym and get to my assigned seat. I walked in next to Tad, who actually looked more nervous than I felt. We were going pretty slowly because it's so hard to get a wheelchair through a crowd, and every kid who passed turned to stare at us. I felt like I had a giant archery target painted on my back or something. It was as though everybody in the school was waiting for me to fail this thing. "Do you have a weird feeling?" I asked Tad. "Nah," he said. "I kind'a have to pee, though. How long is this test, again?"

Lindsey walked by and squeezed my shoulder. "Everything will be fine," she said. I was like, *Did somebody forget to tell her this section of the test doesn't count?* But before I could clarify, they started calling us to our seats. Just like in my dream, Flash McGrath was there, shouting out the names. When he said, "*Al*-per, Jeffrey," I could have sworn the whole eighth grade turned to watch me walk to my desk. Which was just perfect, because you know how much I love it when people admire my stylish limp.

As I fidgeted in my chair, lined up my pencils a million times, and got my calculator perfectly aligned with the edge of the desk, Mr. Laurenzano read us a long list of directions for how to bubble in our names. The kid next to me — Josh Albert, who was *not* sporting any robes or antennae — said, "Dude. How stupid does the state think we *are*?" Meanwhile, I was frantically erasing the line of bubbles I had just finished. Apparently, your name and your birth date go on entirely separate lines.

We finally finished all the filling-in parts, and Mr.

Laurenzano said, "You may now break the seal on Section One of your science packet and begin. You have thirty-seven minutes to complete this section. Good luck, eighth graders."

Just then, from across the room, Tad let loose with the loudest cough I've ever heard in my life and started rolling slowly up the aisle. *Geez*, I thought, *how small could his bladder possibly be?* But suddenly, every kid in the entire room — except me — stood up, slammed in their chairs, and started filing up the rows and out of the gym. What the heck was going on? Lindsey, who'd been sitting two rows in front of me, turned and hissed, *"Come on, Jeff!"* I jumped up and followed — honestly, what else was I going to do? By that point, Tad was wheeling his way across the front, leading a long line of students past all of our teachers, who were frantically putting down their coffee mugs and looking around for some kind of instructions. I guess their riot training was a little rusty.

Well, I thought, *I suppose this explains why everybody was looking at us on the way in.* As Tad reached the door, Miss Palma grabbed the microphone and said, "Students! Students? What are you doing? Come back here *this instant*!" But when I looked at her, she actually looked semi-delighted.

The cries of the teachers followed our procession into the hallway. I wondered for a moment where we were going, but I didn't have to wonder for long. The front doors of the school are only about fifty feet from the gym, and the whole line was heading that way. As soon as we'd hit the hallway, a kind of instantaneous, nervous buzzing had started, like, "Where are we going, again? And why?" "Did you see Laurenzano's face?" "My mom is *so* going to kill me!" But even over that, I heard the thunderous footsteps of Mr. McGrath as he pounded past us up the hallway to stop Tad at the doors. It was like a movie ad or something.

FLASH McGRATH:
THE RETURN

YOU'LL BELIEVE A FAT MAN CAN RUN!

Everybody got quiet then, so that even from fifty feet away, I could hear Tad and Mr. McGrath having a pretty heated argument. This was bad. I had to get up there and calm Tad down before things got even more out of hand. I made my way through the crowd as fast as I could, and reached Tad's side just as he opened the door and Flash bellowed, "Ibsen, if one wheel of that chair crosses this doorway, I *prom*-ise you will be suspended!"

"Fine," Tad said. He reached down and locked the right wheel of his chair, then the left. He looked at me and mouthed one word: *Surprise!* Finally, he slowly, slowly stood up, hobbled past Mr. McGrath, and made his way out into the morning sunlight.

I crowded next to Mr. McGrath, who stood panting by the open door. Tad, holding the railing in a death grip, struggled down the front steps of the school as the entire grade crowded up behind us. A few of the bravest kids started pushing their way out the doors, too, as Tad reached the bottom of the stairs and held up one hand in the V-for-Victory sign. Flash turned to me and said, "You might as well get down there before your crazy friend falls flat on his duff and *kills* himself." I started out, but by the time I got down there, Brianna Slack had rushed past me, dragging Tad's wheelchair. She put it down right behind him. He collapsed into the chair and looked up at her. "Tad," she said. "You *still* stick out your tongue when you walk."

As Tad smiled weakly, I looked past Brianna and realized that there was a TV news van at the curb, and a camera crew charging across the lawn in our direction. The beautiful blond-haired reporter shoved a microphone right up in Tad's face and he started talking. Then, suddenly, Lindsey was right between Tad and me. She put one hand on his shoulder, and reached for my hand with the other.

That was when I looked down at my own hand, and realized I was still holding my calculator. I swear, I must be the lamest rioter in history.

WOW, WHO KNEW THEY GOT NEW JERSEY
NEWS STATIONS IN AFRICA?

TO: dangerous_pie@jerseynet.com

FROM: drum_master@jerseynet.com

Hi Jeff —

I don't believe this: Annette just sent me a link to two
Me-tube videos. The first one is a slick little homemade call
to revolution by your friend Tad, "Produced by" some girl
named Lindsey. I can't believe he had the guts to ask every
kid in New Jersey to walk out on the state tests. And I can't
believe the clip has been viewed 23,000 times! The second
one is a clip from last night's local news there. I suspect you
know the one I mean.

God, Jeff. I've been asking Mom about you all year, and
she keeps telling me you're doing fine. Now I find out that
you might fail math and get held back in eighth grade —
and Tad has cancer again. That must be terribly hard for you.
Plus, apparently you've caused the first riot in the history of

the middle school. And who's the chick with her arm around you on TV? Is that Lindsey? If so, she's kind of cute.

Aww, my little Jeffy's growing up! Do I need to fly home right away and give you "The Talk"?

Actually, I was already sort of planning to come home again next month for your graduation. You probably don't know this, but I had asked Annette not to contact me unless there was an emergency. Since then, I've spent half my time praying for an emergency. I'm sorry, that sounds horrible. But when I saw the message in my in-box today, I was almost relieved — not because of what it said, of course. I just wanted her to get in touch, even though I was the one who had told her not to. So I've been wondering lately why I'm still here.

About the message itself: I thought Tad was really brave to think of that whole thing, and I'm amazed that he actually got everyone in your grade to go along with it. Organizing it through his Myface page and the first video clip was genius, too. This Lindsey girl did a great job with all the video editing effects and all, but I think the real power of the piece was what Tad said. "They tell us to stand up for people who are weak and defenseless, and

225

then they threaten to fail anyone who needs a little extra help?" Brilliant.

And then when he said to the reporter, "I take full responsibility for this peaceful protest. What are they going to do to me anyway — give me cancer?" Wow. He had to know that was going to make big news.

Please tell Tad I'm impressed. He really stood up for you. I don't know if the school board will listen to a bunch of kids, but I do know they're always terrified of the media.

One last thing: Just sitting here at this moment, I decided I *will* come home ASAP. I still don't know whether I've found what I was looking for, but I do know I miss what I left behind. Can you do me one favor? Please ask Mom to get my dark suit dry-cleaned. I want to look suitably fancy for your graduation. I know you'll make it.

Until I get there, take good care of my little brother, OK?

Steven

"Take care of my little brother"? What the heck did he think I'd been doing all year, playing with matches and smoking crack? Plus, what was up with the melodrama? "I still don't know whether I've found what I was looking for, but I do know I miss what I left behind" had to be the cheesiest sentence I'd ever read in my life. It was a cheesy cheeseball, covered with Cheez Whiz and served on a bed of Cheez-Its. With a side of *queso*.

And had he really been asking my mom about me all year? If so, why hadn't he just asked me himself? I understood the part about needing space to decide whether to, like, bond for life with Annette. But I was his brother. Did he really need to be off-limits for a year to figure out whether to be related to me or not?

The sad part was, I was completely thrilled that he was coming home.

The rest of the statewides weren't as dramatic as the first day. On Tuesday, when we walked into the testing room, the principal, both assistant principals, and the superintendent were all there waiting for us. You knew right away this was a big deal, because the principal never came out of his office for anything less major than a terrorist attack.

Or a student revolt.

I was standing next to Tad and Lindsey. Boy, were we popular! Pretty much everyone we knew came up and slapped Tad on the back, or gave Lindsey a high five, or patted my shoulder and said, "Good luck, man." Tad and Lindsey were the heroes of the day. I was back to being the poster child. But it was OK, because when I looked at Tad that morning, I didn't see his puffy eyes or his constant wincing from the cramps. For a little while, Tad was his full-on angry self again. It was nice to have him back.

The second our butts hit the seats, the superintendent started lecturing us. I won't bore you with the details — and I admit I missed some parts because I was distracted by the violent flopping of his hideous toupee — but basically he told us that the science test was "postponed indefinitely." He also said that if anyone did anything to mess up the rest of the testing, he was going to call 911 personally.

Yeah, like that wouldn't make it into the nightly news again: WHEELCHAIR-BOUND CANCER PATIENT ARRESTED FOR FREE SPEECH.

Then the principal tried a softer touch. He never raised his voice, and his "hair" actually stayed in place. He said he "admired our courage" but didn't want to see us do anything to "damage our promising futures." He felt "proud as an American" that we had "exercised our right to peaceful free expression." But if we did it again, he didn't "know what action the state board of education might take against individual students."

Translation: *You've had your fun. Now sit down, shut up, and take the freakin' test. Or else.* Did these bozos think that vague threats were the best way to prepare our brains for three more days of testing? I mean, if they had threatened to make us wear their dreadful hairpieces for a day, *then* maybe you would have seen some seriously motivated students. But otherwise, threats just make kids mad.

I have to admit, though, nobody tried anything for the rest of the week.

After each day of the math section, Tad came zipping up to me and tried to go over every single problem. Of course, I couldn't even remember the questions, much less the answers I had put down, but that didn't stop him from grilling me in detail. I couldn't blame him. He had put more time into helping me with my math than I had ever spent on another human being in my life.

On Thursday, when the entire testing ordeal was over, the principal came into the gym and — right in front of everybody — took Tad away to in-school suspension. I couldn't believe it. First of all, that made twice in one week that the guy had ventured forth from his hidden lair, and second, he still hadn't figured out that Tad was a bad enemy to have.

He probably figured it out the next day, after Lindsey had called all the local newspapers, the TV station, and the state education department. Or after my mom and Tad's mom drove down to the district office and threatened to sue if anything about this went on Tad's permanent record. Tad was back in class by second period on Friday. Going into the weekend, it appeared that Tad had won the free-speech battle. Of course, we didn't know whether the test scores would still be used to fail kids for the year, or what my scores would turn out to be.

But wow, Tad knew how to make a beau geste when it counted. Cyrano de Bergerac would have been impressed. Probably not as impressed as Miss Palma and Brianna Slack, though. Our English class on Friday was one giant Tad lovefest. Miss Palma said Tad was "at one with the Spirit of Liberty," and Brianna called him a hero. He muttered, "Oh, please," but I noticed he was blushing. *Tad* blushing? It was definitely a week for miracles.

At lunch, while we were celebrating with ice cream pops, Lindsey told Tad and me that her dad was going to let her help him edit a commercial in the summer. He had been so impressed with her work on the Me-tube clip that he was even going to pay her for her time. She was pretty psyched. When Tad congratulated her, she caught him wincing. "What's wrong?" she asked.

"Oh, nothing. It's just, you know, a side effect of the Gleevec."

"What's that, again?"

"It's the drug that's supposed to be stopping the cancerous blood cells from multiplying insanely fast in my bone marrow."

Lindsey looked stricken. "Oh, it's no big deal," Tad said. "Your boyfriend here has been through way worse. Like methotrexate, for example. Methotrexate makes Gleevec look like Children's Tylenol. I'm serious. You can ask Jeff."

Lindsey looked at me. I nodded. "But you don't have to take that one?" she asked.

"Not yet. They're saving it for the three days before the bone marrow transplant. That's when they have to completely kill off any cancer cells that are left, along with my entire immune system. Then the doctors just have to drip some cells from my sister's bone marrow into my veins and hope the new cells save me." Just then, the warning bell rang, and Tad pushed back from the table. "Oh, gotta go. Toodles, kids!"

And he was gone. Lindsey turned to me and said, "How can he be so calm about this? He's going into the hospital next *week*. Shouldn't he be freaking?"

I thought about this for a minute, then responded. "Would a *normal* person be freaking? Sure. But when you're going through treatment, you don't think that way. You can't, or you'd die. I mean, my treatment was, like, a millionth of what Tad's been through, and you know what it's done to me. But I know I didn't really flip out while it was happening. There's nothing you can do about it, so you go, and they stick you, and you get sick, and that's it. Freaking out just makes the whole ordeal harder for your mom."

"Is this some kind of macho guy thing?"

"No, it really isn't. I'm not saying Tad isn't brave — he's super-brave. But I've seen three-year-old girls playing Barbies and telling their parents not to cry while they were getting needles inserted in their chest for three hours of high-dosage chemo."

Lindsey said something softly just as the passing bell rang. "What?" I asked.

She put a hand on my shoulder, leaned in, and put

her head so close to my ear that I felt the warmth of her breath as she said, "You're brave, too, Jeff."

I didn't tell her this, but I didn't feel brave. Truthfully, I was scared out of my mind for Tad. I had survived cancer once, which was risky enough. Surviving twice was pretty rare, and three times? Let's just say if this were the Kentucky Derby, Tad would be a long shot.

RIDING INTO THE SUNSET

The week after the statewides was pretty odd. First of all, it was Tad's last week of school. The teachers arranged for him to get his yearbook early, and that Friday was like his own personal Senior Week. Seriously, there was a line at our lunch table of people who desperately wanted to sign Tad's book. When everybody was finally gone, Lindsey said, "Wow, Tad, people are really going to miss you! I mean, until September."

Tad laughed. "Yeah, it's amazing what a little fame and a fatal disease will do for a guy's popularity rating."

Well, at least the glory wasn't giving him a swelled head.

Another strange thing was that I suddenly had some free time. After months of extra math classes, tutoring, and being grounded, I almost didn't know what to do with myself. I rode my bike a lot, of course. I had told so many people about my big ride that I needed to make sure I'd actually be able to go that far without having a heart attack, and with two weeks to go, it was crunch time. I did twenty-five miles a day on the weekend, then alternated between doing ten fast miles and twenty slower miles every other weekday. But even averaging over an hour a day on my bike still left a lot of time.

I felt like I was going crazy. I was all excited about Steven coming home, but every nerve in my body was screaming with alarm about Tad's transplant. So on Tuesday I did what any red-blooded American boy would do: I did my training miles really fast, took a shower, put on a collared shirt, and biked over to Lindsey's house.

She answered the door, looking beautiful in her Angels jersey. Sadly, her team was in first place, but my beloved Yankees were off to a slow start — and she was having fun rubbing it in. "Hi," she said. "I'm just enjoying the thrill of a victorious new season. And what are you up to?"

"Well," I said, "the testing is over."

She gave me a puzzled look.

"And I'm not grounded anymore."

She still just looked at me.

All of a sudden, my heart was pounding and my palms were practically dripping. Amazing how I could ride a bike twenty miles without getting out of breath, but a little old talk with this girl practically put me in the intensive care unit. "And you said you were only breaking up with me until after the tests, right?"

She smiled. "So what are you trying to say?"

I made myself look right into Lindsey's eyes. "So I'm wondering if you still have that mistletoe lying around somewhere."

She didn't, but we made do without it.

The week went by. Tad had his last day of celebrity, and then it was the weekend before Tad's hospitalization would begin. He was under strict orders to stay in his house, and he couldn't see anyone except his parents and his sister. If he got sick it would be a disaster, so I understood the deal. We

IM'ed a lot, which had always been Tad's favorite form of communication anyway. But I felt weird not talking to him before the transplant, so when Sunday night rolled around, I called him on the phone.

"Dude," I said.

"Dude."

"Uh, how are you?"

"I'm feeling rather cancerous today, thanks. And how are you, Jeff? Ready for the big ride next weekend?"

"I think so. You know it's N.B.D., right? All I have to do is climb on and keep pedaling."

"I know. But just in case you need some inspiration, I'll be mailing you a package this week. Just promise me you won't open it until the day of the race, OK?"

"OK. Uh, what's in it?"

"Well, D.A., would I make you promise not to open it if I wanted you to know ahead of time?"

"Oh, good point. Listen, Tad, I just wanted to tell you I —"

"Oh, good lord, Jeff. Don't go getting all emotional on me. I've been getting it from my mom, my dad, my sister, the freaking *mailman* — I don't need it from you, too. All I ask is that you promise me one thing."

"What?"

"Just water the plants for me while I'm gone, all right?"

"You don't have plants, Tad."

"I know. I just always wanted to say that."

"Isn't there anything I can really do?"

"Well, you could check on Yvonne when she gets home from the hospital. Maybe play a game with her — she likes Pretty Pretty Princess. Oh, and you could promise me you'll kick butt in high school."

"Tad, what are you talking about? You'll be there when I get to high school. We're gonna go up there and kick butt togeth —"

"You asked what you could do for me, right? So I told you. IF, for some odd reason, I don't *happen* to be around, just do what I asked, all right?"

I swallowed. My throat felt two sizes too small. "All right."

"Good. Now I have to go get some beauty sleep — wouldn't want to scare the radiologists or anything. Peace out, Cub Scout."

"Tad, I —" I stopped talking when I realized I was speaking to the dial tone.

On Tuesday, Tad's package arrived. It was about the size of a box of tissues, and when I shook it, it felt kind of fluffy. I was dying to know what was in there, but I knew that if I peeked, Tad would ask me about it later and I'd tell him the truth. So I waited.

Somehow, the week passed. I tried not to picture what was going on during Tad's three days of high-intensity chemo and radiation, or what was going through Yvonne's head as the doctors prepared to stick needles into her hip bones and take out more than a quart of marrow. I couldn't imagine what it would feel like to be asked to save your brother's life *twice*.

On Saturday, the actual day of the surgery, I prayed all day. I wished I could burn off some of the nervous energy by going biking, but I never get on my bike the day before the big ride. My parents tried to distract me, and Lindsey even called to ask if I wanted to go to a movie or something, but it seemed wrong to go around having fun while Tad was in the middle of getting his bone marrow transplant. I knew he probably would have said, "Go party, Jeff. Listen, if you were the one in the hospital, I wouldn't be sitting around moping in the window like an abandoned puppy. I'd be out in the streets, living large with my entourage."

But I also knew he would have been lying.

On the morning of the ride, I showered, ate breakfast, and rushed through a long series of stretching exercises my physical therapist gave me when I was in sixth grade. Then my dad wished me luck as I pumped up my tires, checked for my cell phone and emergency money, snapped my water bottle filled with Gatorade into place, and put my bike on the rack behind our minivan.

Just as my mom came out to the garage to spray me with about a gallon of sunscreen and drive me to the starting line, I realized I hadn't opened the package. I zoomed back upstairs, ripped into the bubble mailer, and pulled out — an iPod and a pair of Pull-Ups, like the ones toddlers wear during potty training. There was a Post-it note, written in Tad's nearly unreadable scrawl, on the front of the Pull-Ups:

ALL RIGHT, JEFFY. HERE ARE SOME BIG-BOY PANTS.
PUT 'EM ON AND CRANK OUT FIFTY MILES FOR ME.
BY THE WAY, THE IPOD ONLY HAS ONE PLAYLIST
ON IT. PRESS PLAY WHEN YOU LEAVE
THE STARTING LINE, OK?

I took the iPod and went back downstairs. Mom and I didn't talk in the car. I mean, she tried, but I just wasn't in the mood. I have to say, Mom's always been pretty good at knowing when not to say anything. Of course, once we got to the park where the starting point was, she *did* hug me, and make me promise I'd call her after the first lap, and kiss me on the hair just below my helmet, behind my left ear. But I looked around really fast, and I didn't think anybody had seen.

So that was kind of all right.

I said hi to the various people I recognized from past rides. When I'd started doing this event in sixth grade, Mom had made a couple of old guys promise they'd watch me, but this year at the starting line she just made a little call-me sign with one hand and sat down to watch me go.

The other two times I'd done this, when I was doing only one lap, I'd gone zipping out of the gate at top speed. But I knew if I was going to do the loop twice, it would be smarter to pace myself. I eased my way up through the gears until I slipped into a comfortable cadence. Then I started the iPod. The very first song was an oldie from Eric Clapton called "Tears in Heaven":

> *"Would you know my name*
> *If I saw you in heaven?*

> *Would it be the same*
>
> *If I saw you in heaven ..."*

I knew immediately what Tad was doing to me: It was classic Tad. He had always collected morbidly depressing songs, and obviously he thought it would be funny to make me listen to them during the ride. The next one, as I rode in the middle of the pack through town, was by My Chemical Romance. The song was called "Cancer":

> *"That if you say (if you say)*
> *Good-bye today (good-bye today)*
> *I'd ask you to be true ('cause I'd ask you to be true)*
>
> *'Cause the hardest part of this is leaving you*
> *'Cause the hardest part of this is leaving you ..."*

Tad and I had laughed at the drama of that song a million times, but it put a lump in my throat now. I kept pedaling and got through the song. Track three started just as I started the long downhill ride to cross over the free bridge into Easton, Pennsylvania. It was another oldie, Queen's "Bohemian Rhapsody":

> *"Didn't mean to make you cry,*
> *If I'm not back again this time tomorrow,*
> *Carry on, carry on as if nothing really matters."*

Oh, geez. As I turned with the pack to go over the bridge, I could actually feel tears welling up in my eyes. Then, to my complete horror, I realized there was a pack of girls waving to me from the middle of the bridge. I wiped my eyes frantically on the front of my high-tech moisture-wicking shiny bike shirt, and saw that Brianna Slack was one of them. So was Lindsey. They waved, and cheered me on, and held up a big sign that read, GO, JEFF! MAKE IT FIFTY FOR TAD!

I passed them just as the next song came on:

> *"Na na na na*
> *Na na na na*

Freakin' Tad.

We rode through Easton, and along an old rail-road right-of-way by the Delaware, for about an hour before looping back around. At the end of the first lap, I noticed that the music had ended. I also noticed that my legs were starting to cramp up, so I drank some Gatorade. That helped, but it also made me realize I was starving, so I pulled over, called my mom to tell her I was fine, and got a hot dog at this stand by the side of the highway. That made me fall pretty far behind the pack, but I knew I'd catch them on the downhill back to the river.

I jumped back on my bike and steered with one hand as I wolfed down the hot dog in about three bites. I forced myself to chew each one really well — I didn't want to ruin the ride by choking to death. Then I cranked up to full speed, and got caught up over the next two miles or so. As I crossed the free bridge, I was relieved to see that the girls weren't there anymore. It was my favorite part of a long ride: when you're already tired and crampy, but you're more than halfway done. And it would be so easy to tumble off your bike into the grass and quit, but you know you won't.

I wish I could remember now what I was thinking during those next two hours, because they were the last good hours I was going to have for a long time. But nobody ever tells you in advance when you should concentrate on the good times — that's why you're supposed to try to do it every day. I know, I know: Tad would barf. But it's true anyway.

By the time we made the last big, sweeping turn into the hill that leads to the end of the route, I was in a great mood. The sun was shining, the breeze was great, and I felt like I had really done something important and visible to support Tad. My legs weren't even hurting anymore; I almost felt like I could go around again if I wanted to. I cranked through the gears, and really poured on the speed as the end came into sight.

I looked around to see whether anyone was

waiting for me. At first, I could just make out our minivan in the shade of a tree. Then I saw the outline of my mother, leaning against the driver's-side door. I think she saw me just as I saw her, because she stood up straight, stepped out of the shadows, and started walking over to the finish line.

Maybe twenty feet before I crossed the line, I realized she was crying.

GRADUATION

Well, for what it's worth, I'm here. I never knew it was possible to feel so numb on such a big day. I'm sitting in my hot, sticky gown, trying to keep my big, stupid-looking square hat from tilting and sliding off my head completely. It doesn't help that the metal folding chair I'm on has been baking in the sun for hours. I stare at the sweat-drenched neck pimples of the kid in front of me, but really I'm not looking at anything.

More specifically, I'm not looking around for Lindsey, who's only about seven seats away to my right. I'd be willing to bet a million dollars that she's looking at me, hoping I will glance over there so she can attempt to make me smile. I'm also not looking around for my mom and dad. They're somewhere in the bleachers of the football field, and I know they're reasonably proud of me.

While I'm at it, I'm not looking around for Steven. If I really wanted to find him, I could just turn around and look for Annette's frizzy hair. He's the guy right next to her, holding her hand. But he's probably giving me the concerned big-brother look, and I don't want him to get sick of consoling me and hop on another airplane. If I were feeling anything at all, I'd be glad he's here. He came home a couple of weeks early. Luckily, Mom had wasted no time in getting his dark suit to the cleaners. Suddenly, that thing has been getting a lot of use.

Speaking of which, I'm not looking around for Tad. His parents are here, and so is Yvonne. Yesterday my mother made me stop over at their house with a platter of sandwiches. While I was there, Mrs. Ibsen sat me down at the kitchen table and asked me to do something special for Tad today. I said I would do it. She hugged me and cried.

You're probably wondering what happened with the testing and everything, right? It's pretty ironic, actually. I passed both the English and the math, but the test scores aren't going to count for anything. It turns out that the answer key to the English was all messed up, and when the state auditors started investigating, they found "significant irregularities" in the way the scorers were trained, too. The news channels were all over the story, and the local station even ran a whole story about Tad's role in stirring up public awareness of what the anchorman referred to as "testing run amok." In the words of the editorial that ran in yesterday's paper, "How can the powers that be use this deeply flawed instrument to decide the fate of our children?"

Interestingly, Miss Palma told our class that at least one blogger is saying that the governor's girlfriend is on the board of the company that administered the exams. If that's true, she said that heads will really roll when the state senate has its next session in September.

Big whoop. Tad would have loved this whole scandal, but it's not like he's around to see it. The day after his transplant, just as I started my big ride, Tad went into sudden liver failure — his mom said it must have been something called "acute graft-versus-host disease." She told me the doctors hooked him up to every machine in the place, but it was no use. My best friend's heart stopped at 10:32 AM, probably while I was stopping halfway through my ride to grab a hot dog.

It wasn't even a good hot dog.

The kid next to me grabs my arm and yanks upward. Oh, geez. Our whole row is standing. It seems I've missed all of the speeches, and it's time to walk across the stage. One by one, our names are called.

Mr. Laurenzano is reading the names, and his voice sounds a little bit funny as he clears his throat and says, "And now, accepting both his own diploma and the one earned by our departed friend, Thaddeus Ibsen: Jeffrey Alper."

"Our departed friend?" If he'd heard that one, Tad would have been rolling on the floor. But I'm not. I force my feet to start moving. As I limp up the aisle, I notice that the entire stadium is eerily silent. My heart is pounding, and my lame foot feels like it has three bricks strapped to it, but I make it to the steps at the edge of the stage. I concentrate on lifting each foot as high as I can on the stairs. This would be a bad time for a face-plant.

I glance to my left and almost trip: Every single person — student, parent, teacher — in sight is standing up. And they're all looking right at me. I stop. I can't do this. It's only a few more feet to where the assistant principal is standing, waiting to hand me the diplomas and shake my hand. But I'm paralyzed.

Tad is gone.

Tad is gone.

And then Miss Palma steps forward from the teachers' line. She walks to me, puts one hand on my shoulder, and whispers, "This is your beau geste, Jeffrey. You can do it." And, very gently, she pushes me forward. My feet start moving again. With each step, I raise my knee high and put some glide into my stride. I force my shoulders back. I keep my chin up. I can almost hear Tad say, *Put on your big-boy pants, D.A.*

I have to keep moving. After all, I'm walking for two.

PERPETUAL CARE

I'm sitting in the grass, talking with my best friend, Tad. It's the morning before the first day of high school, and I have a lot to tell him. I've been riding my bike out here every week this summer because even though I can talk to Tad anywhere, this is the one place where I can always hear his voice answering me. My parents have been really, really worried about me. So has Steven. So has Lindsey. Who am I kidding? So has everybody.

I sneeze. Yvonne likes to leave wildflowers right at the base of the headstone. Apparently, I am allergic to wildflowers. There is just so much about this that Tad would find amusing. I've been trying really hard to laugh at the things that would have made him laugh. Sometimes, just in the last week or two, I can even smile without doing it on purpose.

"So, Brother Thaddeus, we meet again."

Hey, have a seat. Make yourself at home. I know it

ain't fancy, but you can't beat the view. At least, from the upstairs level.

"You're not going to believe what I saw in the paper today. The state senate proposed a new law: 'No school shall use a standardized test as the sole criterion for the promotion or retention of individual students.' Isn't that amazing? Dad says he thinks this bill might get passed. Mom says you really kicked . . . well, you know. She even used the word. I almost had a heart attack and died. Oh, God, that sounds horrible."

Meh. You want horrible, you should hear the old guy on my left when he snores.

"And another thing. I got my schedule in the mail, and they put me in grade-level regular math. I've never been in grade-level regular math before."

Yeah, we've all been going through some changes lately.

"My dad is thrilled. I told him it's because of the question he helped me with on the night before the statewides. But he said, 'No, buddy, we have your friend Tad to thank.' I swear, since your funeral, he's been practically displaying emotion."

I'm a miracle worker. No offense, but your dad could have found out how great I am a lot sooner if he had just asked your mom.

"And Steven, too. I got into it with him one night two weeks ago because I told him everything was pointless. He asked me what I was talking about, and I went completely ballistic. I told him your death was stupid and pointless. He said, 'But it wasn't. Tad helped you get to high school. And he made tons of people all across New Jersey stop and think.'"

Well, that was a first. I still can't believe I managed to get people in New Jersey to think.

I snort. "I told him that it was pointless of him to go to Africa and desert everybody if he was just going to come back anyway. He said, 'No, Jeff, it would have been pointless if I hadn't come back. But I did.' I said, 'So why'd you go?' He gave me this whole lecture about that girl Samantha who died when I was in the hospital. I never knew this, but she made him swear he'd always take care of me. I think the exact words were, *Stay with your brother, Steven.* I said, 'So that's why you left for Africa — because a dead girl told you not to? Very nice!' He looked away for a while, and then said, 'No, Jeff, I left for Africa because I stopped listening to her. Now I'm listening again. Dork!' And then he put his arm around me."

Gakk.

"I know, I know." I notice then that tears are dripping down my face and onto the front of my John Lennon shirt. Tad loved John Lennon. "Sorry I'm getting all emotional. Ever since . . . uh . . . May, I've been kind of a wuss."

Kind of a wuss? Kind of a wuss? Dude, you are, like, the Duke of Wussendorf. The Earl of Wussheim. In fact, wherever wusses meet and mingle, your name is whispered in hushed, reverent tones. Now, wipe your nose on Mr. Lennon. Go ahead, I know for a fact he won't feel it.

I wipe my nose. Then I just sit there and breathe in the allergy-inducing wildflower air for a while. When I feel calm again, I say, "I've been going over to your house and playing with, um, the E.R.C."

Yvonne.

"Right. Yvonne. You wouldn't believe how much she misses you. But you know what? She's a cool little kid. I'm teaching her to ride a two-wheeler. She wants to do the cancer ride with me next year. Hey, did you know when she smiles really big, her eyes look like yours?"

Oh, barf. But, Jeff? Thanks.

"No problem."

I sit some more. There's just so much flowing through me. It happens every time I come here, just after I've filled myself up on Tad's biting comments, and just before my butt finishes getting permanently numb. As corny as it might sound, I think about the meaning of life. I felt lost a lot of the time this summer, but at the end of these visits, I know that Dr. Galley is right, that a big part of why we're here is to support the people around us. I know that Steven is right, that journeys aren't pointless if they come with a round-trip ticket. And I know that, even through all of the horrible things that happened to Tad in his three bouts with cancer, Tad's life wasn't pointless.

I know I'll forget all of this later, or it sometimes won't seem as perfectly real and true as it does right now. But then I'll come back. Tad isn't going anywhere. He's right with me in this clearing on the edge of a little town by the Delaware River. And he's right with me in the center of my chest.

So, on this last morning before high school, I think it through one more time. And at least for a moment, I know that the purpose is to keep moving forward. To stick with the people you love, even when they push you away. Even when they're hurting, and especially when *you're* hurting.

I hear a twig break at the end of Tad's row. I turn, and Lindsey is there, walking up the path next to her brand-new street bike. She puts down the kickstand so her bike is right next to mine, takes off her helmet, shakes out her hair, and walks over. She points to a new, yellow sticker on the upper right corner of Tad's headstone and asks, "What's that?"

I know the answer, because I just asked Mrs. Ibsen the same question two days ago. I tell Lindsey that it's a Perpetual Care sticker. It tells the cemetery staff to keep the grave looking nice forever.

Forever. A chill shoots down my back.

"Perpetual Care, huh?"

I nod. "How did you know I was here?" I ask.

"I went to your house first. Your parents' cars weren't in front, but your brother answered the door. Then Annette popped up behind him wearing a bathrobe. I was pretty embarrassed, but they seemed to be cool with it." Lindsey blushes and continues. "Anyway, Steven told me where you were. Are you OK?"

"Fine," I say, smoothing the drenched front of my shirt.

She smiles then, just a little hesitant smile. I think it must be hard for her to understand why I keep coming here. "All righty, then. Jeff, do you want to go for a ride? I'm, uh, a little nervous about tomorrow."

I stand up and hug my girlfriend. Then she takes my hand and leads me back to the path.

About the Author

Jordan Sonnenblick attended amazing schools in New York City. Then he went to an incredible Ivy League university and studied very, very hard. However, due to his careful and well-planned course selection strategies, he emerged from college with a fancy-looking diploma and a breathtaking lack of real-world skills or employability.

Thank goodness for Teach for America, a program that takes new college graduates, puts them through "teacher boot camp," and places them at schools around the country with teacher shortages. Through TFA, Mr. Sonnenblick found his place in the grown-up world, teaching adolescents about the wonders and joys — the truth and beauty — of literature.

Mr. Sonnenblick always wanted to be a writer, too, so one day in 2003 he started the book that became *Drums, Girls & Dangerous Pie*. He was inspired to write the book by the story of one of his students whose brother was battling cancer. In creating the story, he was also inspired by several aspects of his life. Like the novel's main character, Steven, the author really plays the drums, he really went through an incredibly awkward year in eighth grade, and he really was completely spastic around girls until right around his twenty-first birthday. The made-up parts of the book are all reflections of the author's basic philosophy, which is that the world is a tough place, so you'd better be kind and laugh a lot.

Drums, Girls & Dangerous Pie was published to great acclaim and was named to several Best of the Year lists, including the American Library Association's Teens' Top Ten.

Steven and Jeffrey's story continues in the novel *After Ever After*. Mr. Sonnenblick is also the author of *Notes from the Midnight Driver*, which is about drunk driving, lawn gnomes, divorced parents, a unique old man, and a beautiful girl with deadly hobbies; *Zen and the Art of Faking It*, a story about one boy's attempt to fake out his entire school, escape boredom, and get the fearless, guitar-rocking girl of his dreams; and *Curveball: The Year I Lost My Grip*, about how a freak injury causes a high school pitcher to throw his life a few curves. Besides these novels, Mr. Sonnenblick has also written the Dodger and Me series for younger readers and the novel *Are You Experienced?* for older teen readers.

Mr. Sonnenblick lives in Bethlehem, Pennsylvania, with the most supportive wife and most lovable children he could ever imagine. Plus a lot of drums and guitars in the basement. You can find out a whole lot more about him at www.jordansonnenblick.com.

ALSO BY
JORDAN SONNENBLICK

Curveball: The Year I Lost My Grip

Drums, Girls & Dangerous Pie

Notes from the Midnight Driver

Zen and the Art of Faking It